# A CRACKED POT

Tales from the H

ustrated stories from the
ilson, an enigmatic nurse-
midwife from Ireland has left the lush fields of the Emerald Isle
for a sequence of God-inspired personal and medical adventures
amongst the displaced and marginalized women and children in
her traveller's odyssey . . .

This book makes rural development and medical mission explode
into a cameo of colour and converts relief and development into
a pageant of human interest, raw humour and powerful testimony
to a God at this most real in the questions, confusions and
heartache of life at the front line.'

Ted Lankester, Interhealth.

# A CRACKED POT

## Lizzy Wilson

### Illustrations by Conal McIntyre
### Foreword by Martin Goldsmith

with

### Questions for Reflection and Discussion
### by Chris Wright

OM
publishing

Text copyright © 1998 Lizzy Wilson
Illustrations copyright © Conal McIntyre

First published 1998 by OM Publishing
OM Publishing is an imprint of Paternoster Publishing,
PO Box 300, Carlisle, Cumbria, CA3 0QS, UK

04 03 02 01 00 99 98    7 6 5 4 3 2 1

**British Library Cataloguing in Publication Data**

A catalogue record for this book is available from the British Library

ISBN 1-85078-305-5

Cover design by Mainstream, Lancaster
Typeset by Westkey Ltd., Falmouth
Printed in Great Britain by Mackays of Chatham PLC, Kent

FOR MUM
* * * * * * *

My best friend
and spiritual soulmate
who taught me
to reach for the heights.


FOR DAD
* * * * * * *

Your faith and courage
in the face of painful tragedy
have won my deep love and admiration.

# Your Journey

# Foreword

What a pleasure it was to walk with Lizzy across the fields to the hospital where she worked as a midwife. She had been away for some months and it was touching to witness the great warmth with which she was welcomed back – lots of laughter and kisses. Proudly she showed us round the hospital, her pride culminating in her maternity area. We duly admired the brand new incubator for premature babies – until a cockroach marched boldly across the spindly legs of a tiny occupant! We realized afresh that medical work overseas can sometimes require the bubbly sense of humour for which Lizzy is known. When she was a student in my wife Elizabeth's tutorial group at All Nations Christian College, we had come to enjoy her as well as appreciate her loving dedication to the Lord and to other people.

Having taught at All Nations for many years we are in touch with former students all over the world. Newsletters come in considerable numbers, keeping us in touch both personally and also with situations worldwide. But it's always a special morning when the postman delivers an update from Lizzy. Her letters are an experience – vivid, humorous, informative, sensitive and moving. Having read so many of her letters we encouraged her to write this book and now it is a great pleasure to be able to write this foreword in commendation. Lizzy's stories paint a picture of life in all its joys and pains. They will move you to tears of laughter and then to tears of grief as you empathize with those who are hurting. We trust that God will use this book not only to entertain but also to convey to many Lizzy's deep love for people, especially those of the Middle East. In this book the heartthrob of ordinary Muslims comes to us and challenges us to loving service in mission.

Martin Goldsmith.

---

## A 'WEE' NOTE ... FROM LIZZY

This is a collection of true stories. However, in order to protect the identity of those whose stories I tell, I have felt it appropriate not to use their real names. For the same reason I have altered slightly the context and setting of one story.

# With Heartfelt Thanks to . . .

**Martin and Elizabeth** – whose courage in challenging me to commit to paper some of life's richest experiences to date has resulted in this book. Their faithful encouragement, prayerful support and belief that I could do it, has spurred me on and stopped me from 'sitting down' on numerous occasions.

**Chris** – who surpassed her appointed role of editor to become the most *wonderful* encourager and friend. A precious gift along the way.

**Jeremy** – to whose wisdom, patience, gifting and wealth of experience in the publishing world I have had the privilege of entrusting my manuscript.

**Conal and Heather** – shared experiences in refugee Sudan have allowed the heart of my writings to be brought alive with fabulous illustrations.

**Chris** – my highly respected tutor from All Nations Christian College days, whose time and thought have yielded the fruits of the 'reflection and discussion' section of this book.

**The numerous women and children** whose stories I tell. Through the privilege of sharing in your lives I'm a richer person.

**My North African Christian family** – fellow workers who have carried me on a cushion of love and prayer through some of life's most painful moments.

**The many friends** who believe in this 'cracked pot', in its empowerment to write, and most important of all – in the message it carries.

**My beloved family in Dublin** – such a source of shared joy and sorrow. Threads woven in the stunningly beautiful tapestry of our life together. One day we will see the final picture!

**Steve, Helen and James** – so supportive and loving. I love you too!

**Shirley, Penny, Val and Fawn** – treasured spiritual soulmates God has given to walk with me on life's journey.

**The Holy Spirit of God** – who has not only empowered me to write but has opened my eyes to see the world through God's eyes, my heart to feel his pain in our brokenness, and my ears to hear the lament of the master creator – played on the vibrating strings of a seasoned violin.

# Before You Begin . . .
## 'a Peep Through the Curtain'

Six-year-old Faruk peeped through the tattered sackcloth curtain guarding the entrance to his refugee family's home. With his friend Samir close at his side, he strained to adjust his eyes from the brightness of the midday sun to the dark interior of the grass hut. For some moments all seemed black but as his eyes became accustomed to the dim light, Faruk could trace the outline of his mother crouching over the swollen body of his three-year-old sister on the dusty floor. His mother had been like that for so long now that he wondered if she would ever move. Since dawn the whole community had heard only her bitter weeping, weeping for which the neighbourhood women could offer no consolation. The weeping had finally stopped . . . causing him to question whether all was well in that silence. And so he decided to peep . . .

His mother's thin frame and withered breasts revealed the true cost of their flight from warring factions in Eritrea, the long difficult journey over the mountains into Sudan made even harder by the absence of Faruk's father who was fighting their cause with the rebel army. Faruk's sister, Safa, had been a beautiful child before she became sick with the hunger. Petite and fragile, she had no extra resources to fend off illness when it came.

Faruk had taken seriously his responsibility as the only 'man' in the family – carrying his little sister on his back for over half the journey. When they finally arrived at this haven of refuge she was taken to the camp hospital . . . but it was too late. The

*A Cracked Pot*

previous night his mother had returned home in silence with the ashen, bloated body of his much loved sibling and closed the curtain to the outside world. She had wanted to mourn her passing alone. From today the curtain of the hut would stand as a symbol of yet another painful separation in Faruk's life – as if separation from his father and his homeland had not been enough! Behind this ragged piece of sackcloth lay the cold body of his sister awaiting some male folk to carry her out for burial. The knowledge that this was his father's rightful duty filled Faruk with acute loneliness.

He was greatly tempted to use the curtain to shield himself from the piercing reality of the situation. The loss was just too much. Yet there had to be a way forward through this pain. In Faruk's young and tender mind a very strong urge encouraged him to pass through that partition to be united with his mother in her loss. Surely he would find comfort in letting his tears flow with hers! Surely the deep pain of 'living separation' from Safa could be transformed into something positive even beautiful! Surely, surely, surely . . .

There was only one way to find out – so he passed through the curtain.

A glimpse through that 'curtain of separation' is what I desire to give those of you who now embark on sharing in my writings. The curtain touches many different lives in a multiplicity of situations. Behind the curtain are glimpses into lives I have had the immense privilege of sharing over the years: from my upbringing in Ireland to my work as a nurse/midwife in Iraq, Australia, Sudan and North Africa. Lives such as those glimpsed here are ordinarily hidden from us because many are lived in lands and cultures different from our own. They are the lives of people like you and me who walk the path of life's bittersweet experience and endeavour to make some sense of it all.

And so I invite you to journey with me across the frontiers of countries, cultures and religions into the hearts of some of the world's finest people, to feel with me the pain of learning to walk with sensitivity in another culture and of the sore throat that goes with getting my mouth and tongue around its language, to enjoy a taste of my Irish sense of humour and laugh at some of my blunders along the way, to share with me the inevitability of human failure and what it is to face up to my own inadequacies and weaknesses; I invite you to walk in empathy with those whose story I tell and allow yourself to feel the emotions this may stir up.

Finally I invite you to be encouraged by the ways in which a 'cracked pot', in the hands of its master Creator, can make a difference in our hurting world with its kaleidoscope of needs.

Lizzy Wilson

# A CRACKED POT

# 1

# 'Cracked Pot' . . . or What!

A friend once described me as: 'The MIDwife with the MAD personality and the MOD hairstyle!' Yes, I am a nurse/midwife and many people have asked about the road along which I've taken those skills, gained in Ireland and England, to Iraq, Australia, Sudan and North Africa. It's a story some may attribute to the making of my 'Mad' personality which I myself reckon is rooted in the great sense of adventure God has given me. It all started to manifest itself at the age of two – the year marking the 'debut' of my travelling days – and has gained momentum ever since. More about that later . . .

As for the 'Mod' hairstyle . . . if you have never seen me in person you will need to use your imagination on this one. My hairstyle is copied from the Eritrean children I worked with in the refugee camps of Sudan. It is not a feeble effort to be 'mod' or 'punk' but a sign of my identification with those I grew to love during my short time there. Friends and others have described it in a number of ways – a palm tree, a bird's nest, or a 'loo' brush . . . depending on how polite they feel. Basically the sides and back are nearly shaved (just enough hair left to cover my white scalp . . . the original style being designed for brown skin) with an explosion of coconut-oil-bathed curls sitting on the top. Add a pair of 'wacky' earrings and I'm told it goes well with my personality!

I was born in 1961 on Holy Innocents Day – the day when the church remembers the male children of Israel, slaughtered at the hands of King Herod on hearing of the birth of Jesus. My dad named me while Mum was still recovering from the anaesthetic necessary for delivery by Caesarean section. She was later presented with 'Lizzy' – a daughter who would delight in her intimate friendship and share her heart for the vulnerable children of this world.

On Holy Innocents Day the church sends out a special plea to protect the weak from the tyranny of the strong. I responded to that plea at a very young age. My aunty Ruth still tells the story of her visits to our home when I was little. I took great delight in choosing the privacy of her bedroom to show her my colouring book with a picture of the sea-king Neptune in it – complete with big three-pronged fork for catching sharks! 'Now aunty "Roof", this is wicked King Herod who killed all the little babies with his big fork. Wicked, wicked, wicked King Herod who I bash with my umbrella!' This enlightening explanation (accompanied by practical demonstration) answered aunty 'Roof's' question as to why poor King Neptune was covered in perforations . . . a grave case of mistaken identity!

On Holy Innocents Day 1963, my second birthday, Granny gave me a brown doll. It was an oddity in the Irish culture of the day, jealously protected from immigrant subcultures, but Granny was a widely-travelled woman. My heart was filled with compassion for this alien doll – 'Blondy' was the only other doll in my life at the time. Within my little world my foreign doll found acceptance – coupled with a commitment to return her, one day, to her mummy and daddy. My concept of living as a refugee was in its embryonic stages!

Mum informed me that my imported doll was from a sun-drenched land where brown skin was essential protection against sunburn, a land far away where bananas and coconuts grow. And so, six months after my second birthday I started out on the road of adventure to find that land . . . a road of discovery that would uncover the big world 'out there'. As soon as I was sure my older brothers were safely delivered to school and Mum occupied with clearing the breakfast table, I tucked my foreign 'refugee' dolly under my jumper, wriggled my way through the hedge to the next door neighbour's garden, climbed their apple tree and chucked myself over their four foot high wall into the long grass of the meadow. With Dolly now under my arm, my legs were free to run like the clappers – it was only a matter of time before Mum realized I had escaped . . . yet again. Let me see how far I could get this time!

The only things that would stop me in my tracks were a horse without its owner or being caught by our family doctor who sometimes spotted me on his rounds and duly delivered me home – much to my disgust and my poor mum's relief. Nine times out of ten she would be running the opposite way having misjudged my direction. The breakfast dishes would still be in the kitchen sink on Dad's return from work in the evening! But my child's mind saw life as a mission-filled journey requiring a wrestle (with the sharp twigs of the hedge), a climb (up the branches of an apple tree), a jump (over a wall), a fight (through long grass) and a race against time (before I was tracked down). It would be some years before anybody truly understood the importance of that sincere charge. Such were the formative days of working and shaping this human 'clay pot'. Truly I was born to run!

As the years progressed I abandoned the running away in favour of a special relationship with my granny Emily (Mum's mother) – the one who gave me my brown doll. She was a chronic asthmatic and 'chocaholic' who kept her Ryvita crispbread in the airing cupboard and enjoyed it in the late afternoon with banana (classified as exotic fruit in those days) and smoked Earl Grey tea served in a china teacup. School holidays became another journey of adventure as we travelled long hours by train to share in those afternoon 'cuppas' when she told stories of her travels and those of my great-grandfather Jacques. Granny's family were of French Huguenot descent, landing and settling in west Cork, on the southern shores of the Emerald Isle, in search of a better life. She was the only surviving child of the 'Boland' offspring – her five brothers and sisters all having died before the age of three. My great-grandfather Jacques had been a merchant and in his lifetime made the remarkable voyage to China and back. The tall Chinese vases, low mother-of-pearl table, and long embroidered oriental curtains in the sitting room – behind which we used to stow away to the Far East – stood as a constant reminder of this man's amazing adventures. And people wonder where I get it from!

Emily married my tall red-headed grandfather, William, when he was a newly-ordained Church of Ireland minister working in rural west Cork. They lived in a big old rectory set amid a beautiful croquet lawn, flowerbeds bursting with summer flora, ancient tall oak trees perfect for climbing and swinging out of, a rambling orchard, and a mass of bamboo canes for our jungle adventures.

William was a big man with an equally big heart for children – he always had a pocketful of Fox's glacier mints and fruits for distribution after the Sunday morning services. Children just loved him . . . my brothers and I were proud to be the grandchildren of this godly man. I'm not sure, though, how proud he was of us when, as city children in a tiny country church on a Sunday morning, we were not always on our best behaviour. It didn't take much to set us off on a fit of giggles when the organist's dog started to howl in the middle of a hymn – she in total oblivion, being hard of hearing and engrossed in pumping the long oak pedals. Her nose would be touching the music as she endeavoured to see through thick prescription glasses. The congregation of farmers, all clad in their black 'Sundays and funerals' suits and spotless white starched shirts, and their families (hats were the order of the day), seemed unperturbed by the howling of the dog accompanying the whining of the organ – they just sang on as our pew rocked. Not even Mum's and Dad's threats of confiscating our weekly pocket money, due after the service, helped control us. Much as my parents felt embarrassed at the behaviour of the rector's grandchildren, there were times when I was sure I caught a glimmer of a smile on their faces too!

I vividly remember my mum's hat for those occasions – it was Kermit green with what resembled a liquorice allsort sitting on the top. I can't say I was mad about it but had reason to be eternally grateful the Sunday it came to my rescue during one of my grandfather's longer-than-usual sermons. 'Mummy I'm going to be sick . . . NOW!' was the urgent cry from my side of the pew. Mum's immediate reaction, taking off her hat and placing it under my nose, was impeccably timed to receive the contents of a tummy unaccustomed to the extravagance of my granny's 'Milk Tray' chocolates before breakfast! The parishioners, more than aware of her love of chocolate, lavished on her big boxes the likes of which we had never seen before. What they didn't know was that Granny liked only dark chocolate so she saved the boxes of milk chocolates until our next visit. It's not hard to tell where my love of chocolate came from!

Emily and William had five children – my mother was the middle one. At the age of eight Mum was uprooted from the rural life of a funloving child and sent with her older sister to boarding school in the 'big smoke'. There her studies continued until the age of seventeen when she became a medical secretary to a Dublin dentist. All her life she longed to train as a nurse but a near-death experience during a bout of meningitis at the age of fourteen put an end to any strenuous career. Shortly after leaving school she met my father.

Dad was from Northern Ireland – a Presbyterian with strong Scottish roots. He had come to Dublin at the beginning of a career that was to span more than 35 years with the 'Guinness' company. Mum's and Dad's meeting was 'love at first sight' and this north/south union led to marriage at the age of twenty-two. They were stunning people, committed to God and the deep love he had given them for children. Three pregnancies in quick succession produced Philip, David and me! And three we would remain until just after my eleventh birthday when our home was opened to welcome children in need of fostering.

Godly parents, committed to bringing us up in a Christian family, instilled self-worth and security as well as introducing us to the needs of others. We were always taught to be thankful to God for everything we had as well as cultivating a conscience towards those less fortunate than ourselves – both in Ireland and overseas.

'Overseas' came closer to home thanks to our neighbour's two sisters who were Franciscan nuns working in Zambia. When they came home on leave I sat enthralled by their stories of life in the 'bush'. Entrusting my refugee doll to their luggage I asked for it to be returned to the sun-drenched land of bananas and coconuts where they would surely find her mummy and daddy. At the age of five I was sure that one day I would be a nurse and work in that sunny land. In the meantime, I swung out of the sisters' veils singing 'Here comes the bride!' Sensitive or what! On their return to Zambia I wrote them letters confident of their delivery by a little man running barefooted through the jungle with my sealed envelope on the end of his spear. I often worried about the perforations this mode of delivery inflicted but was reassured it would be a 'holey' letter for holy nuns! My concern now turned to this courier's bare feet – I committed myself to sending him a pair of my dad's shoes the next time the Sisters came home on leave. The seeds of adventure in my life were being nurtured.

Growing up in a home often described as: 'a railway station at rush hour' by day, and 'the lighthouse of Dublin bay' by night, was truly an education. A world in need came streaming to our front door day and night as Mum offered of her best to the travelling community and many others. On returning from school it was often necessary to climb over a family of 'travellers' devouring tea and sandwiches on our front door step with mur-murings of 'God bless ye luv' as we passed. We always gave Mum a hard time about the numerous black plastic sacks full of secondhand clothes which came in and out of our house. She was never allowed to forget the few occasions our jeans and jumpers were accidentally given away while waiting to be claimed from the clean washing pile. Mum was a giver with a big heart always putting the needs of others before herself. She challenged us to do the same.

Dad committed himself to working long hours to keep the family afloat financially. His dedicated support of Mum and all her diverse activities was matched only by his incredible tolerance, as he never knew what would be there to greet him when he arrived home from work in the evening. Even Dad would never send away empty-handed a caller asking for 'a little help'. His speciality was tins of baked beans and processed peas but he was somewhat 'miffed' when hedge-clipping season came along and the offending articles were discovered stuffed into our thick front hedge! Yet he always proved a willing chauffeur when night callers (usually a group of 'travelling' children) asked for a lift home to the foothills of the Dublin mountains – complete with dog stuffed under a jumper.

Other people came to our home in search of Mum's listening ear and counsel – we knew well the need to respect the invisible 'Do not disturb' sign on the sitting room door when such sessions were in progress, sessions ministering to the bruised, the hurt, the sick, the depressed, the rejected . . . those in deep despair. That world 'in need' later crossed the threshold as many hurting children came to share in our family life. It was a home well known for its elastic walls and elastic meals served with the welcome of: 'Our house is clean enough to be healthy and dirty enough to be happy!' Families of travellers, children from broken homes, international students far away from their families, visiting speakers to our local church, African mission partners on a cultural exchange, senior citizens for Bible study groups, our Roman Catholic neighbours for ecumenical prayer meetings, children in search of a holiday club, children, children and more children . . . they were drawn to our house like magnets. Even the waifs and strays of the cat community knew where to come!

At the age of eleven my parents made the decision to start fostering babies. And how I loved those little ones! Tearful 'goodbyes' watching a baby pass on to the next stage of life's journey were somewhat eased by the delivery of two more in immediate need of love and care. One out and two in . . . the numbers increased. The coming and going continued as short-term care led into long-term fostering and in some cases adoption. Our family expanded as we adjusted to these new brothers and sisters, many of whom were scarred and traumatized. Not only were we taught willingly to share our possessions with others but we were now challenged to share our parents with children whose emotional poverty caused them to be very demanding at times. Nor was the life of the hurting child in our home the sole focus of attention – concern always extended to the child's kin, for a traumatized child was often the product of a traumatized mother.

My understanding of people's profound emotional and spiritual needs was increasing. Offering to meet such needs required a deep level of love, commitment and sacrifice and my parents sensitively introduced each one of us to the source of that love . . . a love which won my heart at the age of twelve.

In the context of that love I could fully appreciate the intimate friendship I would share with Mum, a precious soul mate God gave me along life's journey. In latter years I would share that intimacy with Dad when the sharp pain of bereavement drew us together in a special way.

At seventeen I finished school and embarked on my nursing career – my eyes still set on working overseas. Children deprived of basic health care pulled my heart strings as I committed myself to respond in whatever way I could. However much my family upbringing had taught me about people's complex needs, those early years of nursing in the inner city areas of Dublin were a raw shock to my system. They were very tough years of forced transition into the role of highly responsible adult with people's lives in my hands. The new phenomenon of grey hairs stood testimony to the deep demands of my chosen profession. These years were accompanied too by a promise from my home church to send me to the wilds of Sudan where the elephant grass rises high above one's head and Dinka tribesmen hunt with long spears. In the middle of this war-torn land the building of a health clinic was being financed and someone had had the wonderful idea of sending *me* to run it! The idea was in conflict with my childhood dreams of sun-drenched bananas and coconuts. I was left feeling inadequate and afraid at the prospect.

So, soon after I qualified as a nurse, with my backpack on standby, I jumped at an opening to work in Iraq instead. I was on the run again – this time in the direction of the Middle East where sand and date palms replaced elephant grass . . . phew! At the vulnerable age of twenty-one this was my first assignment overseas and ironically after all, to a country at war. My relief at apparently dodging a hair-raising appointment in the elephant grass of Sudan was soon replaced by an unfolding comprehension of the amazing way in which God had allowed my feelings of inadequacy and fear to drive me to this ancient cradle of civilization. For there, away from the security of family and a culture in which I felt 'at home', he allowed me to begin uncovering the true riches of Middle Eastern culture. He started to show me his heart for these people with their profound needs, deep pain and suffering. He opened my mind to grasp the foolishness of war and my emotions to shed tears with those of whom it demanded a high price. Most of all he challenged my ability to trust him to meet ALL my needs in the face of wherever he would lead me in the future. No longer would I be driven by feelings of inadequacy and fear but by a deep sense of dependence on him and his divine direction.

I would never find physical separation from my family easy, being a 'home bird' with a travel bug. Little did I know that my time in Iraq was to be the beginning of many years working in the Arab/Muslim world, and that in time I would train as a midwife and relish the delights of intimate contact with its mums and babies. God's infinite wisdom, or maybe his Irish sense of humour, would one day direct me back to the Sudan after all – to a country and refugee community that would hold a very special place in my heart. My childhood refugee doll had provided an important 'stepping stone' into the real heart of where life's journey was leading me!

And so my 'clay pot', worked on by the hands of the skilled potter, had grown and been shaped over the years. With that process certain to continue another was gaining momentum, for I was also destined to be a 'cracked pot' – a pot beyond a 'Superglue' sticking job! Over the years I would suffer many cracks leaving me amazed at how I am still together at all. Cracks . . .

Cracks from knowing what it is to be hard pressed on every side by the overwhelming demands of refugee Sudan . . . the poor, the powerless and unmarried pregnant of North Africa.

Cracks from being totally perplexed emotionally by war in Iraq with its costly suffering; cracks from being perplexed intellectually by the need to learn two new languages; cracks from being perplexed professionally when the skills I had to offer proved insufficient.

Cracks from persecution when my taking a stand for the weak of this world has not proved too comfortable for some of the strong.

Cracks from being struck down by ill health and personal loss. A painful and fragile back tired of the physical demands of life, a breaking heart paying the price of painful 'goodbyes' through tragedy and heart-rending forced separation.

> *I have been hard pressed but I have* NOT *been crushed.*
> *I have been perplexed but I have* NOT *been in despair.*
> *I have been persecuted but* NOT *abandoned.*
> *I have been struck down but I have* NOT *been destroyed.*

For Scripture affirms that my cracked pot is a vessel that carries around in it a treasure – the life of Christ shining through my imperfect mortal body. In that case, the more cracked the pot is, the more brilliantly the treasure can shine from within! So . . . crack on, crack on!

# 2

# Gunpowder: the Fragrance of Death

'Allah Akbar! Allah Akbar!' (God is great! God is great!) The call
rang out in waves across the sprawling city of Baghdad bathed in
muted sunset shadows. The heat and dust of the day settled with
the sun as the melodic chanting of the muezzin, calling the faithful
to prayer, rang out across the Iraqi capital in the direction of
Mecca.

The beauty of the 'Egg and Eye' mosque was unique. Its
elliptical body of gold and turquoise tiles gleamed in the sun's
departing rays. The 'eye' soared high into the evening sky – a half
moon waiting to take its place amongst the starry host. This focus
was held in place by the adjacent minaret, its stonework revealing
the fine masonry of Iraq's most skilled craftsmen and its intricate
detail complementing the stunning simplicity of the 'egg'. Truly
this mosque reflected something of the professed greatness of
Allah, a greatness which hundreds of the gathered faithful now
united to declare.

On that Friday evening marking the close of National Martyrs'
day, this throng of followers of the Muslim faith was composed
largely of the city's elderly menfolk; the younger and healthier
men were heavily engaged in fighting their cause on the Iran/Iraq
border. As I watched I became conscious of four different kinds
of unity represented in the scene before me.

Firstly – the unity of those who had gone through the extensive
purification procedure of washing, before dressing in ritual

garments of white cotton. Barefooted they presented themselves before Allah in neat rows standing shoulder to shoulder.

Secondly – the unity of those whose life in the trenches allowed them only half a rusty can of muddy water in preparation for Salat (prayers). All clad in well-worn, seasoned khaki uniforms and high-laced muddy boots, they too presented themselves before Allah. Machine guns in hand, facing east in ditches that had long since become 'home', they maintained a fixed watchful gaze, always on guard. The circumstantial lack of physical unity in the sense of standing close to others was replaced by the unifying hope that 'Allah the most merciful' would understand their situation. After all, it was for his cause they were fighting this holy war.

Thirdly – the unifying declaration of faith in shouts of 'Allah Akbar!', vibrating the walls of the mosque and ringing out once more into the evening sky. At the front a chanting of the same words would develop into a battle-cry as each man struggled to believe once again in Allah's greatness, his readiness to grant them victory in what they perceived to be a 'jihad' (holy war) against Iranian forces. Their voices too rang out in the direction of the setting sun whence their enemy came . . . and whence their victory would surely come.

Finally – the unity of submission to a powerful force in the person of President Saddam Hussein, belief in the wisdom of his leadership being essential to fight another day. All stood unified in the hope that one day this bloody fighting *would* come to an end. Meanwhile there was a high price to pay in pursuing that hope. And pay they would.

There is something significant about being reminded of your Irish roots whilst working overseas. St Patrick's Day 1984 marked my seventh month working in the Iraqi capital. My inbuilt desire for adventure had brought me, aged twenty-one, to this ancient cradle of civilization. To a country at war with its neighbour, Iran. To a nation drained from the effects of that war and ailing economically. To a people and culture very different from my own. To a people in physical need of my nursing skills and the specialist care we offered as a hospital. To a people in emotional need of contact with the outside world from which they felt more and more isolated. To a people in spiritual need of a God who is compassionate and loving as well as great.

And in Baghdad how easy it was to feel isolated, living and working in the context of an expatriate existence! So it was a real treat to finish work on 'Paddy's Day' at 3.30 p.m. leaving me free to prepare for an evening concert being given by a group especially flown in from the Emerald Isle. It was definitely an occasion to spend time choosing the right evening attire and applying some make-up. After all, the tell-tale signs of a long eleven-day stretch at work could do with a bit of covering up!

Anticipation of a good evening had been building up and was soon to reach its climax . . .

As I strode light-footed across the hospital grounds towards the main entrance, my bubble of elation burst as a khaki-green military coach blocked my path. My gaze rested on the driver engaged in deep discussion with our nursing officer and the sister of the orthopaedic/cardiac surgery unit on which I worked. Even as I watched, casualties in various states of consciousness and unconsciousness were being unloaded from the makeshift ambulance. My mind flashed back to rumours two days before of Iranian forces launching a new offensive just 50 kilometres from Baghdad. Blocked transmission of the BBC World Service usually meant something was up. The rumbling of mobilizing tanks through the streets of Baghdad the night before last now made sense. No need for more questions. Within ten minutes my silks had been replaced by a white uniform and I was striding, now heavy-hearted, (make-up still intact – whoops!) back across the hospital grounds.

The smell of ignited gunpowder, the stench of festering wounds, and the moaning of mutilated men almost bowled me over as I stepped back into the world of work that evening. Within minutes our ward had been transformed and now resembled a railway station at rush hour with stretchers coming and going, beds being shuffled to accommodate new arrivals, staff rushing here and there with blood transfusions and bottles of intravenous fluids in hand. Ward aids piled mountains of shredded, mouldy, bloodstained khaki uniforms into the incinerator

for burning while surgeons assessed each individual casualty –
prioritizing places on the operating list that would span the next
days, nights, weeks and months. The familiar homely atmosphere of our ward had been replaced by the stress of an intensive
care unit now accommodating twenty critically-ill front line
casualties. Tonight it had been humanly impossible to stick to
our hospital ethics of treating only civilian casualties. It was well
known that local government hospitals were lacking in basic
nursing and medical care. Overcrowding meant that many patients there were just given corridor floor space amongst the filth
and grime, only to await death and a final release from earthly
misery. Tonight there would be no hope of even corridor floor
space in local hospitals as casualties piled in from North and
South. The huge gap in specialist referral care had been the very
reason why we had come to work in this capital. To refuse
military casualties on this occasion would have meant inevitable
death for many.

I was assigned room six into which Tahir and Ahmed were
welcomed. For many weeks the walls echoed with the hum of our
voices as we struggled to communicate, with moans of discomfort
and delirium as the young men woke from surgery and anaesthetics, with cries of pain as open wounds were dressed and redressed,
with bitter sobbing as they grieved over lost limbs, with shrieks
of terror as nightmares were relived, all punctuated with occa-
sional laughter as lighter moments were also shared. Room six
would often be a pit of misery as physical and emotional pain cut
deep. Yet it was to be a place increasingly marked by a divine
presence bringing a tangible expression of a great God of love and
healing.

If my first impressions of Tahir and Ahmed were of fear-filled
eyes, their first impressions of me could well have been of a
shocked and horror-stricken face. Shock at their teenage bodies
mutilated so young – Tahir having yet to celebrate his sixteenth
birthday – and full of potential. The horror at cutting off bloodstained uniforms and bandages to uncover the most nauseating
sights – gaping wounds, fragmented bones, oozing infection,
scavenging maggots, implanted shrapnel and burning gunpowder.

I found it hard not to retch as festering garments were exchanged for clean hospital gowns and wounds cleaned and wrapped in sterile white dressings. After emergency surgery Tahir and Ahmed were nursed to recovery between clean cotton sheets and cushioned from unbearable pain by powerful medication. Gradually they relaxed into a growing sense of a more secure environment -- reassuringly far from the horrors and fear of the battle front, an environment in which they could be their age and not forced before their time into a manly role, gun in hand. They found themselves in an environment in which they could continue their childish exploration of the meaning and appreciation of life without being compelled to blast that God-given life-force out of another.

Ahmed's legs had paid the high price of accidentally stepping on a landmine. The same blast left his entire trunk oozing with burnt skin which needed many dressings and careful attention. Thankfully the cruel encounter had left his youthful, almost childish, face unscarred. Timely surgery saved his left leg but sadly was unable to salvage the right. Early signs of creeping gangrene left only one option . . . amputation. It was emotionally painful for Ahmed to come to terms with the loss of his leg, yet as time passed I felt a little confused at his mounting joy, a complete contrast to the initial bitter sobbing. In a quiet solitary moment he explained to me that Allah had been good to him in taking his leg away, for now a return to the front would be impossible as he was classified as unfit to fight. His experience of war had been short, sharp and shattering but now there would be freedom to enjoy the rest of his days with his family. He dreamed on.

Tahir's legs and arms came out the worst from his unfortunate encounter – shattered bones and muscles ripped open by the butt and bayonet of an enemy rifle. Long tedious operations left many internal and external metal pins and plates holding everything in the optimal position for healing. Plaster, bandages, pulleys, weights, numerous cords and metal frames filled the bed, swung from the bed and tied him to the bed. Boy, was he at our mercy in those early weeks!

The laboured humming of the air-conditioning became a familiar melodic accompaniment to the peace and tranquillity experienced only at 3 a.m. on night duty, when the tide of frantic daytime activity had finally ebbed. At that time a moment could be snatched to gather one's thoughts and listen to the sound of 'silence'. And how noisy that orchestra of silence was! The high-pitched soprano shrill of night-time grasshoppers could send one on a wild goose chase. It was incredible how invisible they always remained considering the amount of noise they made. Then there were the guttural croaks of frogs and toads wallowing in the delightful evening watering of the surrounding parched gardens. I must admit to having a soft spot for these tenor and bass singers! The symphony was supplemented by those patients whose physical and emotional wounds left them moaning in and out of sleep. Their alto hum was frequently punctuated by the startling cries and shrieks of those reliving the nightmares of front line experience. For them the nights were endless and they longed for the flow of daytime activity to return.

It was during one of these treasured 3 a.m. moments that Tahir's call bell attracted my attention. In the dim light of the night's half moon I approached his bed, drawing close in order to hear his voice without waking Ahmed. A request for painkillers was not uncommon at this hour of the morning. Yet tonight's request was a deviation from the norm: 'Lizzy, there's a body beside my body that needs medicine!' came his soft response to my presence. Confusion and lack of understanding were not unusual as I worked across a language and cultural barrier. This was one of those moments – at 3 a.m. I am not at my best intellectually! 'Have you pain Tahir? Would you like something to ease it?' was my feeble attempt to make some sense of the situation. 'No Lizzy, it is the body beside my body that needs medicine!' With that Tahir raised his left arm to reveal a squashed and rather breathless four-legged furry creature lying in his armpit!

Pursuit of the mouse had helped to fill some of those dark 'awake' hours experienced by many on our ward. The unassuming, curious creature passing through the door of room six in

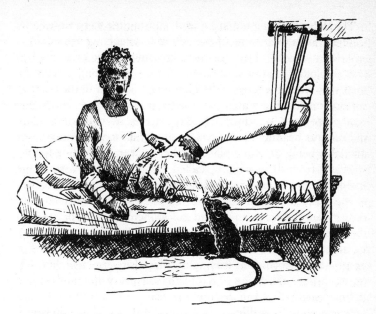

search of a midnight snack, soon caught Tahir's attention and determination. The challenge of pinning down the rodent escalated thanks to the complete immobilization of Tahir's four limbs. After some time this agile furry friend climbed onto the foot of Tahir's bed and started to skirt the rope suspending his plastered left leg from an elevated pulley – through which another rope passed to a 5-kilo bag of sand. He enjoyed a time of sightseeing on the scaffolding before descending the rope to sit on the knee of the plaster. A long hop to the right uncovered leg provided opportunity for Tahir to attempt a catch by bringing his knees together. Unfortunately the slow response of the plastered limb anchored to weights, gave the mouse the moments he needed to wriggle free. 'Better luck next time!' Patient waiting finally saw him remounting the plastered leg and exploring Tahir's abdomen and upper body. An open left armpit became an attractive warm haven. As soon as the mouse entered this crevice and started sniffing around, Tahir put every ounce of strength into drawing his arm right into his side. BRAVO, victory at last! And how Tahir

*A Cracked Pot*

delighted in catching me 'off guard' causing me to be noticeably startled! Such were some of the lighter moments we shared.

Life in war-torn Iraq became increasingly male-orientated. It was the lot of men to cause and sustain the fighting. It was the men who filled the streets, the men who gathered in the mosque for prayers five times a day. It was teenage boys and grown men who made up the continuous Friday afternoon stream of new and old recruits heading for the city's railway station, the only ticket available being one for a place on the ghost train heading for the southern front. It was rightly called the ghost train owing to the fixed gaze of the emaciated uniformed soldiers travelling on her to the dreaded world of daytime nightmares. Those final steps of return were taken in an attitude of aloneness and reflection on their responsibility to fight in the name of Allah for their country. Family warmth and bonding remained behind the closed doors of home, these expeditions leaving no place for sentimentality. Filtering through the streets of Baghdad from every direction, united in both destination and destiny, the years of war told their story on those gaunt faces filled with sadness and pain. This train would carry them away from their families to a cause and ultimate hope that might mean a separation extending far beyond that day.

If it is men's lot to cause and sustain war, then it is women's lot to sacrifice their menfolk to it. A woman's place in this Arab Muslim culture seemed clearly defined. Her role in life was primarily to marry, please her husband, bear him children, and run the home, caring for all in it. On marriage a man honoured his bride with a gift of gold jewellery which offered financial security for her should he die or leave her for another. Women treasured this wedding gift all their days understanding only too well the importance of safeguarding it lest troubled times lie ahead. Pregnancy and childbirth followed in hope of honouring the family with male infants. Nothing was gained without labour and pain – yet this was her crown of honour as a wife and mother.

In this country at war, the definition of a woman's place became sharper and narrower. Sharper in the increased pain of its experience and narrower in its ever more limited freedom. A woman's place in the home was even more strictly enforced with an unspoken (yet well understood) twenty-hour street curfew for women allowing only four hours in the morning for shopping. The long hours of 'purdah' at home were eased by a television transmitting endless programmes affirming the glorious victories of Iraqi forces over the enemy. Further draining of the country's resources saw an increased emphasis on the honour gained in presenting wedding gold as a gift to Allah in the name of a holy war. So broadcast accounts of glorious victories on the front were now followed by footage of long lines of veiled and unveiled women presenting their only financial security to the Iraqi President. The final hours of the evening's entertainment were filled with heart-rending pictures of long lines of silent black-veiled women receiving medals from the President. A medal made of some type of plastic honoured the men sacrificed to Allah and their country. The uniqueness of a woman's ability to give with her body through childbirth, and with her financial resource from marriage was shrewdly recognized by this male-dominated society. In women lay the potential to support this war already in its fourth year.

Tahir's successful surgery and good healing resulted in re-mounting fear as wounds closed and pins were removed. Our rejoicing at his final rising from the bed onto crutches was contradicted by the increasing anxiety in his face. Not even the joyful singing of 'Happy Birthday' as cake and Coke marked the end of his sixteenth year, masked his fear. He knew the days were numbered before a return to the front would be enforced. As soon and as long as he was able to walk and hold a gun, he was needed.

The day of Ahmed's final discharge from hospital found me rummaging through the laboratory's deep-freeze in search of his amputated leg. It wasn't unusual for a family to request surgically-removed body parts, holding to the practice of their burial in what will be the final place of rest for that person. Yet handing over such a conspicuous limb proved particularly difficult at a time when discretion was always necessary. Not even an extra-large black refuse sack left much to the imagination!

The trickle of departures marked by Tahir's and Ahmed's discharge from hospital gradually developed into a constant flow of 'goodbyes' as all twenty exceptional clients were waved off. The tide's turning was marked by a certain restoration of normality as the more friendly family atmosphere returned to our unit. Yet the walls remained poignantly impregnated with the smell of gunpowder and odour of burning flesh. The 3 a.m. orchestra of silence was now augmented by the haunting moans and cries of wounded spirits reminding us of the cost many paid in the pursuit of hope.

Ahmed's joining the prayer line in the 'Egg and Eye' mosque was accompanied by thankfulness to a great Allah for his new life of freedom.

Tahir's rejoining of the prayer line in the bunker was accompanied by pleading with the same great Allah to preserve his life and give him courage. His request may only just have reached the heavens when all was over in a single blast.

In time a veiled mother dressed in a black 'yashmak' joined the line of many awaiting the distinction of being presented with medals in exchange for the lives of their loved ones blown up at the front. It was a professed honour to be martyred in this way.

Tearful moments of waiting gave Tahir's mother time to remember: she had been in this place before, honoured for presenting her wedding jewellery to the Iraqi president in support of a final and lasting victory in the war.

Only four weeks earlier she had relived the painful honour of sacrificing her only son to the battlefield once again. No amount of honour now bestowed could stem the flow of her inconsolable tears stretching over days and nights. In the depths of her mother heart she knew that her fragile son would never return.

And now the honour of a medal. A plastic medal in place of a physical body to grieve over. A plastic medal in place of her son's soft voice and infectious laugh. A plastic medal as a token of a life martyred in the name of Allah. A plastic medal symbolizing pain, loss and separation.

As she pondered, she reflected on the irony of her response as a woman in Iraqi society. A bizarre thought crossed her mind: 'Could it conceivably be possible that her jewellery had financed the buying of the Iraqi grenade, decidedly off-course in its throwing, which had landed and exploded at the feet of her dear son?' A thought she would do well to forget.

As the setting sun marked the close of another day, the unifying cry 'Allah Akbar!' came ringing out in the direction of Mecca. A cry of affirming belief for those in the mosque, a battle-cry for those at the front, and a piercing cry of painful separation for a mother whose only son had been sacrificed in the name of a holy war . . . the honour of such a sacrifice reflected in a plastic medal. Could this great Allah really be a God of plastic?

# 3

# With the Flick of a Switch

I almost had to pinch myself to believe that I was really seeing, with my very own eyes, one of the seven wonders of the modern world. How many times had I revelled in its beauty on postcards or in travel brochures! The dream of beholding it for myself one day now became reality as I stood gazing across Sydney harbour. The Opera House was truly stunning! Sitting in splendour at the water's edge of this vast natural port – perhaps the biggest in the world – its smooth white-tiled body basked and bathed in the afternoon sun. Yet at the same time it seemed like a graceful swan waiting to glide across the water, her rounded feathered wings held in poise. Poised too were the different segments of the Opera House's body – unified in shape yet varying in size. Like freshly-piped white meringue, their contours and peaks sat smooth and inviting to touch . . . Oh, just to be able to run a finger along the outline and then lick it! Yet I knew this was something to be relished through seeing and not touching. The joy of hearing what was on offer inside this spectacular building would be a treat to savour in the coming weeks.

Now to unpack my backpack and really experience life in this Australian city. Not only was my arrival in Sydney the halfway point on my seven month 'round-the-world' jaunt, but it was also the beginning of a time set aside to enjoy getting back to work as a nurse – all with the added bonus of lining my pouch for the trip home. And how far away home now seemed to me 'standing on my head' in Aussi! Even the stars were unfamiliar. In the three months since I had set out from Dublin on a bleak January night-ferry to England, my travels had taken me through the spirit of the Orient and the heart of this vast country: from the reclining Buddha of Bangkok's royal palace and the opium-smoking hill-tribes of the Golden Triangle where Thailand, Burma and Laos meet, to the pulsating heart of colonial Britain's last bastion – Hong Kong. From the Portuguese flavour of Macao, to the vastness of Chinese plains scattered with people, ducks and bicycles. From Singapore's Raffles Hotel set in the upmarket, litter-free, sweaty jewel beyond Malaysia's equatorial tip, to this vast island of Australia. From the surfing waves of Perth, to the ghost gums, kangaroos, koalas and soaring eagles of the outback. From a hot-air balloon over Ayers Rock at dawn, to the leech-infested rain forests of Cairns. From the seasoned Italian fishing boats and giant clams of the great barrier reef, to the vines and flowing wine of Adelaide. From Melbourne's four seasons lived in one day, to Sydney's spectacular harbour. I was happy to have arrived.

The warm security of a bed to sleep in for these coming months was accompanied by a sudden unwelcome sense of lost freedom. The return of professional responsibilities came wrapped in a restricting white starched uniform, nylon stockings and stiff black leather shoes, all of which demanded a temporary 'goodbye' to the liberating baggy shorts, T-shirt and soft sandals of a back-packer enjoying the lazy life of a coconut island in the gulf of Siam. Nothing like coming down to earth with a bump! Knowing that my journey home would take me through New Zealand, the South Pacific islands and the west coast of the United States, helped cushion the blow a little.

Sydney harbour was a sight I was privileged to enjoy in the days to come, thanks to the hospital's panoramic view of the city's skyline. Harbour Bridge stood as a gateway into the heart of this metropolis made up of the most amazing assortment of people from every culture and walk of life. My time here was going to prove an education! Platform 1 of Central Station was *the* place to be on a Saturday night for free entertainment rivalling a London West End comedy show. The everyday diversity of people set the scene, with their lives acting the drama . . . it was live *and* reality.

However much I had relished the freedom to travel during the previous months, love for my work came before all. Enfolded in a special God-given fondness for newborn babies, I needed little encouragement to pour my heart back into it. And so I was welcomed as a member of the medical team working on the special-care baby unit of one of the city's big hospitals. My soft Irish accent mingled with the twang of Australians and New Zealanders as our gentle experienced hands cared for sick and premature babies representing the many social classes and cultures of Sydney's society. It was demanding work.

Interwoven with the hard slog were lighter moments of fun and laughter. I soon resigned myself to being the source of great amusement as my cultural innocence created new Irish jokes by the minute. I was accustomed to the Irish telling 'Kerry' jokes, the English telling Irish jokes, Canadians telling 'Nufi' jokes and Europeans telling Polish jokes, but it was quite a shock to arrive in Sydney and discover them telling jokes about *us*! Incredible how the fame of the Irish reaches even these far-away shores. I can't deny my guilt in adding to the collection: 'Did you hear about the Irish backpacking nurse who put two boiled eggs in the microwave to heat them up? With the 'ding' she opened the door and they duly exploded in her face. She spent the rest of the morning in Accident and Emergency having eggshell extracted from her scalp!' Rather unfortunate, if you ask me.

And then there was the response to my innocently asking why certain sheepskins, which we placed under the babies to prevent pressure sores developing, were pink. The unit sister was surprised I had never seen pink sheep before. To be perfectly honest there were a lot of things I was seeing in Sydney for the first time in my life. Viewing Platform 1's offering on a Saturday night confirmed my growing belief that in Australia *anything* was possible . . . even pink sheep! More fuel to keep the coals burning. They were certainly getting good mileage out of me.

As the days passed, my range of Irish expressions had to be modified. I was soon told that, 'How's the crack?' and 'What are you rooting for?' had other – undesirable – connotations in the Aussie vernacular so I needed to drop them for the more

polite: 'How's life with you?' and 'What are you looking for?'
I was almost afraid to open my mouth . . . and as for eating
boiled eggs . . . well . . .

It was important to laugh now and again in a unit which could
be a source of great encouragement when all went well, but also
a source of great sadness when a baby died.

Watching a determined one-pounder fight for his life and make
it was *such* a delight. These little scraps would sit in the palms of
our hands, resting a head on the tip of our fingers. Mastering the
art of letting us know exactly what they wanted, they certainly
kept us on our toes. Holding their breath and setting off the alarm
bells on the ventilator when life got a bit boring and lonely, was
a game they delighted in . . . especially at break times on night
duty when a nurse was running the show alone! Such characters
packed into just the weight of a bag or two of sugar – as my mum
would say.

Dang was the weight of nine bags of sugar and seemed totally
out of place amongst the 'premmies' filling the remaining incubators in the intensive care alcove of our unit. He gave the impression
of being half-reared and completely outsize for this environment.
Yet every breath that filled his lungs since birth had been carried
out by a life-support machine. The rhythmic rise and fall of his
chest was the only movement apparent throughout his otherwise
motionless body. He was a beautiful child with rounded limbs,
chubby fingers, Chinese eyes, and a mop of jet-black spiky hair.
My instinct was to stroke his little hand and gently awaken him
but in my heart I knew his limp frame would not respond. Heavy
sedation had been necessary to control excessive convulsive fitting
manifest soon after his entry into the world. For now he needed
to sleep as we held onto the hope of a spontaneous opening of his
closed eyelids . . . one day. Maybe he was waiting for the moment
when his mother could be at his side stroking his hand.

For Lai painful daylight hours followed an emergency night
delivery by Caesarean section. The happy Vietnamese mother of
two healthy girls had come into hospital excited at the prospects
of an addition to her little brood. Ten years had gone by since the
delivery of her youngest daughter, and both she and her husband

Phan longed for a son to complete their family. Those years of yearning had been spent as 'boat people' in Hong Kong harbour awaiting a place to settle and rebuild their lives far away from the terrors of their homeland, Vietnam. Once settled and secure on Australian soil, they decided to try for the complete fulfilment of their dreams . . . a son. Comforted in the knowledge that this baby was to be delivered in the luxury of an Australian hospital, and not at home in Vietnam with the aid of a traditional birth attendant, Lai relaxed into the security of her privileged environment. A good diet during pregnancy had ensured a healthy-sized baby ready to push its way out. Maybe he was even too robust for her petite frame – deprived of essential vitamins through the hardship of her childhood years.

The hours passed as labour progressed slowly. Despite good contractions the baby's head sat over Lai's pelvis like an out-sized egg balanced over an undersized eggcup. A medical decision concerning the safest mode of delivery was being made when the sack of water holding the baby burst – a very normal progression of labour. But on this occasion a loop of umbilical cord presented itself in the flow of amniotic fluid, so heralding the onset of an obstetric emergency. The unborn child's only oxygen supply was now being pinched between Lai's pelvis and the bones of its skull. It was 1 a.m. Every minute seemed like an hour as emergency preparations were made to deliver this baby by Caesarean section. Despite the need to open up an operating theatre, call the anaesthetist and obstetric registrar, Dang was born 21 minutes later, the handsome son Lai and Phan had hoped for. Alas, those 21 minutes of oxygen deprivation had left their mark on this little life.

For almost the next fortnight Lai's hands joined forces with ours to ensure the best care for her precious son. Through the long hours spent poring over Dang's incubator a special friendship was born between this Vietnamese refugee mother and the Irish backpacking nurse – both so far away from their respective homelands. Lai's tear-filled eyes pleaded to be shown a way to reinstil health and vitality into this little body. As the days passed her nervous hands slowly gained confidence to become the gentle, yet firm hands needed to massage the tired limbs of Dang's frame. Flaccid muscles craving energizing stimulation absorbed hours of her motherly attention. Faithfully consistent in her committed care, Lai's private unintelligible chatter with her little one in Vietnamese often broke into the melodic lament of a mother's longing heart: 'Oh! Son of my heart, flesh of my flesh, bone of my bones, for ten long years I have carried you in my breast and in my dreams. Through the perilous flight from the country of our forefathers to a life of hardship as homeless people on the waves of the China sea. A promised place of refuge and liberation in Hong Kong's harbour turned into long years as prisoners locked in our own dreams. Gazing day after day through the iron bars of a porthole to the outside world my eyes envied those who walked in liberty on the mainland. Night after night my heart cried out to the creator of the starlit universe as I rocked in my bunk. I even gave up the hope of one day being free and longed for home. Home with a life sentence of hard labour and possibly even death for our rebellion seemed better than dying a nameless refugee, a number amongst thousands, in a strange hostile land. Through it all the promise of one day holding you in my arms brought renewed hope, a hope that increased with the joy of finally being welcomed to settle on this great island at the end of the earth. The painful yet joyous nativity of one dream led to the birth of another – precious YOU. How my breasts long to suckle you! How your father longs to entrust to you his family name! How your sisters long to show you the new world to which we have come! How we all long to see your smile, know your chuckle and give you our love.'

But Dang responded to none of her words. His limp and motionless body was sustained by tubes and machines. A tube passing into his lungs provided the essential airway for a ventilator to breathe for him. A tube into the veins of his umbilicus was the means by which oxygen levels in the blood could be regularly checked and the electrolyte balance maintained through infusion fluids. A tube through the nose into his stomach afforded a channel through which precious breast milk could be given at two-hourly intervals. Yet another tube offered assistance to an

impotent bladder in its eliminating of waste products from the body. The only vital function Dang carried out unassisted was the beating of his heart.

It was true that we had at our fingertips all the modern technology necessary to sustain some of the main bodily functions – but the breath of life lay in the hands of God alone. As I asked the triune God of Christianity to touch little Dang with his healing power and to reach out to this refugee family in their heartache, Lai struggled desperately with her concept of suffering. A follower from birth of the Buddhist faith she was well acquainted with its philosophy concerning the pain and misery of human existence. According to Buddhism, suffering has its roots in human desire and ignorance which in turn result in rebirth. Good and bad deeds in previous lives will determine one's reincarnated state in this life. Release from suffering can only be attained when the cycle of rebirth is broken through clearly outlined persistent human effort. Only then can the way be opened to a place of *nirvana* – the much sought-after state of ultimate happiness. Needless to say, with this philosophy governing Lai's perspective of her sad situation, she lived under a heavy blanket of guilt. Locked in a state of self-condemnation and blame she seemed incapable of hearing, let alone believing, that a God of love and compassion wept with her.

As the days progressed, with tubes still helping to sustain Dang's life, all sedation was withdrawn to determine his true level of consciousness. Lai's maternal eyes watched in deep longing for any sign of reawakening . . . perhaps a curling toe or a twitching eyelid. Nothing! Only the rhythmic rise and fall of a ventilator-driven chest. When Dang was 12 days old certain brain death was confirmed by scan. All hope of his ever waking up slipped through our fingers. On day 14 Dang's little family congregated to say their goodbyes. A quiet room provided the privacy needed to share these painful moments together. Dang was washed, then dressed in a cotton nightgown and blue cardigan before the final removal of the tubes and the flicking of the ventilator switch. Wrapped in a warm blanket, his still-pulsating body was given to his parents and sisters to cuddle for the first and last time. Over the next hour they stroked his sallow skin, washed his face with their tears, sang their heartfelt lament until his body became cold and his heart beat its last. I was an emotional lump of jelly!

The day the ventilator was turned off I found myself back at the water's edge in Sydney harbour. Once again a mother's grief was cutting through me. In only a matter of days my backpack would be filled again and my eyes set towards home. Bidding farewell to the certainty of a roof over my head, I found it hard to be excited about the adventure that lay before me. However much a return to baggy shorts, T-shirt and open sandals might prove physically liberating, and the release from professional responsibility a relief, my heart was heavy as mentally and emotionally I carried Lai and Dang with me. An unexpected sharing in another mother's painful loss had caught me off guard in what had been planned as a backpacking trip of fun and adventure. How quickly I had been brought back to the heartthrob of human existence – suffering and living separation.

That night a long-awaited visit to the Opera House was my farewell treat in this amazing place. In the heart of this modern wonder I listened to famous Australian ballads telling how Sydney's great port grew from a secret gem tucked away at the ends of the earth to become a prosperous cosmopolitan city. I heard how in the early nineteenth century during the reign of Queen Victoria, English ships with tall masts and tough captains brought thousands of poor Irish political prisoners (inflammable matter according to Her Majesty!) to the penal colonies of these shores . . . many never to return. Convicted of crimes such as 'utterance of unlawful oaths' in a country of pathetic, unheard people starving and dying from the potato famine – these men, women and children were packed like sardines and chained in the bowels of ships heading east to the very edge of loneliness. Those who survived the five months of hell with its dysentery, pneumonia and scurvy arrived to a new life in a weird and wrong place. As hard workers they became the backbone of Australia's economy. Despite their miserable misfortune these Celtic people managed to hold onto the belief that every cloud has a silver lining – however black with thunder and lightning, and pregnant with rain it threatened to be.

These ballads also sang of an Irishman's great ability to laugh at himself. And so today the unique Irish sense of humour is woven into Sydney's society. The fond telling of Irish jokes now made more sense!

In some way my awakening to my fellow-countrymen's arrival on this vast island brought me closer to Lai's plight as she was carried to these shores. From those who arrived on the slim-bodied, tall-masted nineteenth-century ships sailing under the command of Her Majesty the Queen of England, to those who came on the broad-bodied, square-sailed sampans of the China sea whose 'sharks' offered a pricey new life of hope to fleeing refugees – all had been driven out of their homelands before arriving on these shores.

On the journey home my backpack carried wee mementoes of my travels: a silk sarong from Thailand, shortwave radio from Hong Kong, marble chopsticks from China, oriental spices from Singapore, opal from Australia, woollen kiwi socks from New Zealand, T-shirt from Fiji, volcanic rock from Hawaii, and a Mickey Mouse from Disneyland. But the souvenirs I would carry with me all my days were those of the people I met along the way – enriching me with their life's experience. Lai was no exception!

Lai fell pregnant again soon after Dang's death. In the seventh month of pregnancy she went into premature labour giving birth to Nhu by emergency Caesarean section owing to apparent distress *in utero*. Nhu weighed in at one and a half bags of sugar relying on a ventilator to fill her tiny lungs with every breath in those early weeks. Modern technology helped her win the fight for life and this time they made it! Her family were thrilled. Their gratitude was directed towards a God whose compassionate love was slowly winning their hearts. I rejoiced with them halfway around the world.

In the years to come, my life's journey would take me to England, Sudan, France and ultimately North Africa. Those years would be filled with midwifery, tropical community health and medicine, French and Arabic language-study, cross-cultural mission training, and most of all, a deepening in experience of lives living separation. Through those years simple letters carrying news of Lai and her precious family came from 'down under'. Life as refugees in a strange land was far from easy but they never gave up the fight. I did my best to encourage them along the way. Their letters brought encouragement to me when the unexpected shock and pain of losing my sister in a car accident struck. They had already walked that path. And then there was a truly priceless phone call six months after a freak accident had claimed the life of my mum and left my dad smashed up in hospital. For months after hearing about Mum and Dad's accident Lai had saved money each week in the hope that one day she would be able to afford to phone me. It had been eight years since we shared the pain of Dang's death and now her totally unexpected voice on the other end of the telephone line cut deep into my heart. Her words were profoundly simple: 'I just wanted to hear how you are doing. To thank you once again for being there for me when Dang died, for showing me the true compassion of God. I want to assure you that I am here for you in the pain of your loss. After all, isn't that what friends are for!'

# 4

# Snapped Cords

She was Kaltouma, or card holder number 35,553 on the records of the United Nations High Commissioner for Refugees. Her stunningly beautiful physical features and melodic mother tongue belonged to the luscious rolling hills of Eritrea in northern Ethiopia. Yet she found herself gripped by the unfamiliar, unyielding pains of childbirth in a grass hut in the sparse, semi-desert plains of an overcrowded Sudanese refugee camp.

Every night her dreams carried her back to the warm security of her loving family in Eritrea. Every night she could once again breathe in the fresh mountain air, listen to the laughter of children playing barefooted along the mountain paths, and hum to the bells of the goats skipping through the meadow. Every night brought a new hope that one day warring factions would lay down their arms and peace would open the door of return to such a dream.

But for two nights an unwelcome intruder had stolen Kaltouma's dreams. In their place pain had given her long, sleepless, dark and lonely hours to agonize over the reality of her present situation. Physical pain had brought her in touch with the deep emotional wounds of forced separation from her family and homeland. Her marriage to Faizal in the camp the previous year had been incomplete without her mother and sisters. Tonight there was a marked absence of their emotional and psychological support supplementing that already offered for two days and nights by women in the refugee community. However loving and

caring Faizal proved, childbirth was women's business allowing
no place for a husband's support. Kaltouma had long since begun
to despair at the length of this painful ordeal. 'And how long was
it going to continue anyway?' Would she ever live to see the child
her body was trying so desperately to deliver into this world? The
unanswered questions faded into a blur of exhaustion and numb
submittal to this unyielding and all-consuming force.

At ten o'clock one night the community leader of Kaltouma's
block of grass huts sent the hospital driver to collect me from our
'on call' compound. His ultimatum was clear: 'This girl has kept
us awake with her howling these last two nights. If you don't do
something, it will be up to me to ensure that the rest of the
community sleep tonight.' My sympathy went out both to Kaltouma in her painful state of prolonged labour and to the community trying to sleep in unsoundproof grass huts. I decided to
take the labouring mother and the traditional birth-attendant
caring for her to the hospital building. At least there Kaltouma
could direct her howls in the direction of the open desert and I
would be in a better position to care for her if complications
loomed.

Our route to the hospital took us on a slight detour across some
bumpy ground. The antiquated Toyota Landcruiser's loss of
shock absorbers and total absence of suspension, made our ride
even more exciting and productive. It wasn't called 'The
Boneshaker' for nothing! There was no need to ask Ali to take
this now familiar nocturnal route of ours. He sensed by the tone
of the case that a bit of a 'shaking up' wouldn't go amiss and might
ultimately help labour along. A wink of the eye served as an
unspoken agreement we shared. After all it was in his best interests
too that this girl delivered soon without complications. None of
us fancied the idea of a long night drive to the nearest referral
hospital some three hours away, provided permission to leave the
camp was granted by the police.

My body started to tell me how much it would appreciate
seeing bed before dawn. It had already been a long sweaty day
and the familiar sight of a full moon and glittering Milky Way
belonged to the minutes of sky-gazing from under my mosquito

net before slipping into a deep slumber. I had a sneaking feeling such a vantage point would not be on tonight's agenda.

The moon served as a welcome source of illumination in a grass building with a small paraffin wick as its only other source of light. Placed on the ground to the side of the delivery table where Kaltouma now lay, the wick's rays unobtrusively outlined the form of her labouring body. Prolonged labour was due to the baby's position – lying with its back to Kaltouma's back. This made the labour not only tedious but also excruciatingly painful. Every contraction pushed the baby's head down onto the base of its mother's vertebral column and exerted pressure on the spinal cord. Kaltouma's bloodcurdling howls with each contraction were an accurate reflection of how painful that process was. I felt myself becoming frustrated once again at the language barrier which prevented me from giving moral support through words of encouragement at a time when I had no other pain relief to offer. Language and cultural barriers stopped me from really getting alongside these mums in labour.

Kaltouma clung tightly to the hand of the traditional birth attendant whose presence thankfully seemed to comfort her. Traditional midwives made up the workforce caring for the camp's women in childbirth. They worked independently of us (occasionally attending training days we held for them) and delivered approximately 80 per cent of the camp's babies. They were highly respected in the community and played a very important role in women's health. A lot of effort went into relationship-building with these 'wise' women. Yet tonight I had a strange feeling of being the 'outsider' whose presence symbolized something of an intrusion. Maybe the traditional birth attendant felt threatened by my involvement and the family might now refuse to pay for her services. I consoled myself knowing tomorrow would provide an opportunity to catch up with Fatma – whom I fondly referred to as 'the million dollar midwife' because of her sari patterned with wads of one hundred dollar bills. She was as blind as a bat and it never ceased to amaze me that she continued working in this capacity, often managing complicated cases. Maybe she had felt quite capable of continuing alone in her care of Kaltouma as it had not been her cry for assistance that drew me into the picture. But the case had been handed over to me which meant I was now responsible for the life of this labouring mum and her unborn child. Under that weight of professional accountability I made a conscious effort also to encourage Fatma's ongoing care in my overall management of Kaltouma and her baby.

On examining Kaltouma at midnight I was confident we would have a delivery by 4 a.m. I racked my tired brain cells in an effort to put together an intelligible sentence of encouragement and reassurance. There is a lot of truth in the expression, 'When the emotions go up, the intellect goes down'! Physical exhaustion was fast helping my emotions gain momentum and propelling my intellect down the scale to below zero. My offered verbal encouragement with every contraction came in the form of, 'Don't worry Kaltouma, only four more hours to go and it will all be over.' I felt 'chuffed' that I had thought of something and my pronunciation even improved with the frequent repetition. After some time howls increasing in volume and intensity made me question the benefits of my encouragement. Maybe a foreigner speaking pathetic Eritrean was more of an irritant at a time like this. I decided to reserve my offer of encouragement for every *second* contraction.

From my vantage point on a tiny stool only a few inches off the ground, I could observe Kaltouma's contracting and relaxing abdomen. Every five minutes the uterus would tighten, squeezing pain receptors of nerve endings and sending signals flying off to the registration centre in the brain. Signals received loud and clear triggered a dynamic expansion of the chest. A jet of air then resounded with the vocal cords in the throat causing impressive vibration of all the skull and facial bones. The vibration seemed to be transmitted through the scalp to the hair roots and then rippled to the tip of each strand of hair. Kaltouma's hair-do (which now resembled something akin to a flattened Christmas tree) was in total synchrony with the process. The crescendo came as fully-vibrating, resounding air erupted through the oral cavity in the form of a blood-curdling howl. My counting of 'howls' started to fall into a pattern. Each howl came at five minute intervals; every second howl provided the opportunity to offer my words of encouragement; every sixth howl prompted me to assess foetal well-being by listening to the baby's heartbeat, and gave me an opportunity to improve the circulation to my increasingly numb posterior. Every twelfth howl marked the passing of another hour. It was now 1 a.m.

In a desperate effort to keep my tired eyes open, I directed my attention to the paraffin wick. A multitude of night-flying insects had already been drawn to the brightness of its flame. This week marked the plague of stick insects with long elegant wings. From dusk the ground opened its pores releasing one by one numerous air corps of flyers. For hours the process continued until the night sky was thick with these airborne fighters. They joined the hosts of faithful mosquitoes who graced us nightly with their presence. I watched them zooming in close to the flame, many too close, singeing their wings and falling to the ground. A little lizard soon emerged from behind the grass mat that served as a partition. I watched his stomach swell visibly as he fed on these fallen casualties. Twelve howls marked the passing of another hour.

As labour progressed Kaltouma's contractions became more frequent and increased in intensity. My words of reassurance continued as before with an adjustment of counting to three-minute intervals. The brightness of the paraffin wick started to burn my weary eyes encouraging me to rest them for a while. I was an expert at micro-sleeping, having gained plenty of practice during my backpacking days. My thoughts went back to the night I had spent sleeping standing up in a Thai bus. Such emergency sleep is not renowned for its quality but it does serve an important purpose at times like this.

At 2.30 a.m. my drooping eyelids were jolted open by a shriek accompanied by Kaltouma sitting bolt upright in the bed with great force. The silhouette of her labouring body with 'flattened Christmas tree' hairdo, was as impressive as the shriek she had just let out. Her soft, moist, brown facial skin reflected the light of the paraffin lamp. Before I had an opportunity to enquire what had provoked this unexpected display of anguish, she suddenly dramatized a heart attack, falling flat on her back as if dead. Thankfully Fatma's conclusion of definite sudden death was soon overridden by my assessment of the situation. Kaltouma in a state of total despair was hoping a dramatized heart attack would provoke a real one and put an end to her misery. I felt I was on the verge of having one myself! It was 3.15 a.m. before my adrenalin levels calmed down allowing me to slip back into the pattern of howl-counting while resting my weary eyes and nurturing a now totally numb bum on a hard stool. Micro-sleeps were well and truly taking over as my body screamed for rest. I put my brain into 'auto pilot' leaving it responsible for monitoring my patient, while I leaned over, adopting the foetal position on the narrow stool, and gave way to my body's desperate plea for sleep.

At 3.30 a.m. I awoke with a start. My brain was telling me that something was not right. My ears were struck by an alarming silence. The howling had stopped and gentle murmuring had taken its place. I jumped to my feet as the murmuring gave way to pushing and grunting sounds. Yippee! the baby was finally coming. My excitement was not shared by Fatma who seemed a bit put out that I had woken up. The baby's head was fast advancing into her hand leaving me to occupy a position of 'observer'. I was very happy for Fatma to continue in her role as birth attendant, wanting to keep to a minimum my intrusion on the care she had given from the beginning. Within five minutes the baby's head was delivered prompting me to check there was no umbilical cord wrapped around its neck. My finger soon came up against a double loop now tightly encircling the neck and threatening strangulation of the baby. 'Stop pushing' came my forceful command as delivery of the body could not go ahead until the cord had been clamped, cut and unwound – a very simple yet important procedure requiring a bit of co-operation and patience. But Kaltouma was clearly not going to cooperate, especially as the command came from me and not her trusted traditional birth attendant. Fatma in her turn was in no mood to be patient and started forcefully pulling the umbilical cord over the baby's head. She seemed irritated by my apparent interference.

'Please Fatma, don't do that as there is another way' came my plea as alarm bells continued ringing in my head. All words fell on deaf ears causing the cord to tighten even more around the baby's neck. The pulling continued until the cord gave way and snapped. Success on Fatma's face conflicted with horror of all horrors on mine. This half-delivered baby was no longer attached to its inner life line supplying him with essential oxygen through the placenta from its mother's bloodstream. In place of life-sustaining oxygen he was now losing precious oxygenated blood through a snapped cord. Every second counted as rotation of the shoulders facilitated delivery of the body. Lots of congratulations and embracing between blind Fatma and relieved Kaltouma accompanied his first cry. For me frustration mingled with panic as I fumbled in the shadows of the paraffin wick to clamp off a haemorrhaging umbilical cord which had detached at the skin junction of the abdomen. Three carefully placed sutures were the only answer followed by a big sigh of relief as the bleeding stopped. 'Thank you God for the safe delivery of this new life into the world.' I was now in a position to offer my congratulations to a proud mum who joined Fatma in blissful ignorance of all the drama. It seemed inappropriate to shatter this moment of joy with a pathetic attempt to explain in another language what had just happened. Would they believe me anyway?

Tying up loose ends before returning home at dawn, I found myself pondering on the profound statement 'Our journey from the womb through the birth canal to the awaiting world is the most perilous journey we will ever take.' I wondered if this little Mohammed would ever know how perilous that journey had been for him. Would he ever fully appreciate how a snapped cord had threatened his life before he had ever had a chance to live it? Or would the perils of the life that lay ahead of him become so all-consuming that the dangers of this night would pale into insignificance?

Amid all these unanswered questions one thing was certain. This snapped physical cord would not be the only snapping of a cord likely to threaten Mohammed's life in the future. Yes, birth had resulted in detachment of a physical cord of contact with his mother's body. But there was also an unseen emotional cord of bonding which had developed *in utero* and which would continue to grow in strength as Mohammed nursed at his mother's breasts and grew. And there was also the deep spiritual cord of bonding that would develop and grow. This cord would bind Mohammed to the culture and religion into which he had been born – his identity as an Eritrean, born a refugee in an alien land yet deeply bonded to his homeland, and his identity as a follower of the Muslim faith. Future sickness, famine, war, and death would all threaten to sever those cords.

Six weeks later I met Kaltouma walking through the refugee camp proudly carrying Mohammed on her back. Her stunningly beautiful face, neatly plaited hair and warm voice radiated an air of relaxation and contentment in her new role of motherhood. She was delighted with her son and already seemed far removed from the horrors of her long and painful experience of childbirth. My delight at meeting mother and son was soon shattered by an unexpected bombardment of disapproval concerning my competence as a midwife. I was thrown into a state of acute concern as I urgently tried to piece together the few words I understood. After much repetition the accusation became clear: ' You're no good as a midwife. You kept on telling me not to worry as I only had four weeks to go before I would deliver. Praise be to Allah whose intervention saved me from death as I delivered that same night! You see you're no good as a midwife.' As she walked away in disgust repeating 'You're no good as a midwife, can you imagine only four weeks to go Kaltouma . . .', the source of the accusation became amusingly clear. In my sentence of encouragement to Kaltouma throughout labour I thought I had reassured her not to worry as she only had four more hours to go before she delivered. But a language blunder had confused the word Sa'ah (meaning hour) and Sabou' (meaning week). 'Don't worry Kaltouma – only four more weeks to go and you will have delivered!' Very reassuring at a time of acute distress! Her mounting despair, incessant howling, dramatized heart attack, and lack of confidence in me as a midwife, all made sense in the light of this very unfortunate blunder.

Once again I found myself pondering, this time on the great purposes of God interwoven with my pathetic humanity. It was God who had ensured my presence at Mohammed's birth enabling me to deal with his snapped cord. It was God too who had endowed me with an Irish sense of humour allowing me to laugh at myself when I made such stupid language blunders. It was to him now that I turned with this discouraging snapped cord of trust and professional confidence.

I would never know what Mohammed's life would stand for but I had a deep sense of God's presence at his birth – a presence that extended an invitation to Mohammed from the Giver and Sustainer of all life, to reach out and receive the gift of an unsnappable cord of life offered through Christ.

# 5

# A Healthy Child is a Picture of God, a Hurting Child of his Son!

The sun rose, a ball of fire behind the hundreds of dawn-silhou-etted grass *tukuls* coming into view on the horizon. Home to forty-seven thousand Eritrean refugees from northern Ethiopia, the *tukuls* stood as a symbol of life in the lifeless semi-desert waste which stretched over a hundred kilometres east from the last inhabited Sudanese village to the Eritrean border. The next stop after the camp was 'no man's land', where only members of the Eritrean People's Liberation Front (EPLF) circulated. As long as their struggle for independence from the Ethiopian government continued, this would remain home for those who now awoke with the rising sun. Another new day – to be lived far away from their homeland – had dawned.

From the huts rose little pillars of smoke joining the dawn haze which rested over the camp. These pre-dawn fires were used to brew tea and generate some heat in these cold winter mornings. The sun now rising above this smouldering charcoal blanket, casting out shafts of spectacular orange and yellow light, prom-ised to be a source of heat for the coming daylight hours – an important assurance as charcoal was expensive, in short supply and considered an extravagance in common daily use.

Our journey into the refugee camp at dawn was often an inspiring experience, a start to a day guaranteed to hold plenty of unexpected 'growing' experiences. Travelling in from the local

Sudanese town where we lived gave us at least 40 minutes to focus our thoughts on the daily demands of the environment in which we had come to work. We were a small team of Christian development workers drawn from England and Ireland in response to the immediate needs of these displaced people for basic health care. A doctor, midwife (me!), three nurses, two community development workers and an administrator made up our team, a team which held full responsibility for the overall health care of the camp's inhabitants (preventative and curative) along with its community development. Every day was filled with new challenges, frustrations and disappointments . . . I focused once again on my appreciation of these minutes travelling, minutes when I could just 'be', before the busyness of the day erupted around me.

We sped along the 30 kilometres of dusty track to the outskirts of this vast settlement just in time to 'drink in' the glory of the rising sun. This morning's sunrise was no exception in its beauty and grandeur. The sun's faithful rising stood as a promise of renewed daily hope . . . the hope of new life, of sustained life, and the unquenchable hope of a better life to come. Each day of camp life was lived with this deep sense of hope. Without hope all was lost.

I asked Ali, our driver, if I could be dropped off prematurely in order to complete the remaining distance on foot. I relished these moments of walking into a new day with the rising sun, especially when it marked the beginning of a stint 'on call' in camp. This expanse of grass *tukuls* would now be my base for seven days and seven nights as I walked into a new week of handling obstetrical emergencies . . . eek! Goats grazing joined children squatting in the wasteland at the camp's entrance. Shouts of '*Kawagiia*' (foreigner) welcomed me as they all went about their daily toilet. My treasured moments of tranquillity were over . . . I had arrived!

On arrival my first stop was a grass hut in the hospital compound to which we welcomed pregnant mums for antenatal visits. It also served as a base and meeting place for the local midwives with whom I worked. Rachida (a senior Eritrean midwife) was there to greet me with a rundown of the new lives she had delivered over the previous 24 hours. She joined me in some fire-brewed sugary tea before leaving on her daily round of visiting newly-delivered mums. Rachida was a fairly well-trained capable midwife whose experience had earned her the position of supervisor over the other trained midwives employed by us. She was their first point of contact when they ran into difficulties, leaving me as their second. She played an important role in the teaching and training of traditional birth-attendants whose unsupervised practice was greatly sought after by the majority of labouring women. We worked well together.

Alamine (one of the community health visitors) soon arrived with an update of unregistered births overseen by traditional birth-attendants during the previous 24 hours. I mused over the fifteen new babies whose first sunrise would have been that which I had drunk in as we drove into camp that morning. In them lay the fulfilment of hope placed in new life. Then there were the four whose earthly lives fell short of the rising sun. Under the dark shroud of night they had squeezed their way into the world only to slip out of it again. Unfortunately such fleeting visits were all too common and now an accepted part of refugee life. I made a note of these (often avoidable) deaths with a view to visiting the mums and the birth-attendants who had cared for them.

With the perils of the night and its dangers of childbirth past, it was to the hope of sustained life of the mother that I now turned. Pregnancy and childbirth took so much out of these refugee women whose resources were very limited or even nonexistent. Food rations were far from adequate and malnutrition rife. Life for these mums was tough. I often referred to them as – 'the poor, the powerless and the pregnant'! Sharing their hope for a better life to come, I searched desperately for ways in which such a vicious circle could be broken. Their wellbeing and that of their offspring lay heavy on my heart.

It was late afternoon when I finished my work and set out to locate Rachida. She provided me with a summary of women known to be in labour and we took some time discussing the management of these cases. Reassuring her of my availability should she need me, I retired to our 'on call' compound and waited . . .

The sun's setting was as spectacular as its rising. At six o'clock the fiery ball dropped out of the sky and sank into the desert. From points dotted around the camp little pillars of smoke soon began rising to form tonight's smouldering charcoal blanket. The sun took with it the warmth of its caressing rays and the chill of the night which lay ahead gave me goose pimples. Supper of cold tomato paste omelette washed down with gritty tea from plastic beakers was consumed huddled around a *kanoon* (charcoal fire). The paraffin lamp soon attracted the nightly squadrons of flyers delighting in the warmth of human skin and the nourishment of human blood. I took refuge under my mosquito net and tucked myself into the security of my bed. The expanse of the starry heavens was mine to behold as I drifted into a deep sleep feeling at one with creation and its creator.

It must have been 3 a.m. when the headlights of an approaching Landrover woke me with a start. Rising from bed with my torch I soon located my necessities bag (for whatever lay ahead) and joined Ali in the front of the car. Rachida had sent him with a scrap of paper bearing the message, 'PLEASE COME. I NEED YOU!' Our journey took us through rows and rows of dark sleepy *tukuls* until we eventually arrived at the outskirts of camp. Male members of the family we were called to had been posted as watchmen along the way. They guided us to the *tukul* where an anxious Rachida awaited our arrival. However much I dreaded the still-unknown complications awaiting me on these expeditions, I really savoured the moments of walking into the dim light of these grass homes. It was a sharing in the intimacy of family life under the cover of night. I was the most welcome visitor drawn into the heart of the family during one of life's most important passages. I felt very privileged to come so close to the heart of these people and their culture.

But tonight there was a contradiction between the joyful presence of newly-delivered life and the heaviness of the prevailing atmosphere. My attention was drawn to the limp body of a young Eritrean girl called Wahiba – the first-time mother of a beautifully healthy baby boy. The source of concern soon became clear as Rachida retraced for me her steps through the care of a normal labour, uncomplicated delivery, and the subsequent collapse of the mother who now failed to respond. It seemed appropriate to whisper within this sombre dark atmosphere, a paraffin wick the only light. I had a deep sense that this delivery was nothing to 'shout about' owing to the obvious poor state of the mother's health.

On clinical examination this young mum had all the signs of a massive stroke. My heart sank as the long-term consequences of such a diagnosis flashed before me. In the short-term mum and baby needed to be transferred to the camp hospital for treatment and observation. Two members of the immediate family travelled with us to provide the much needed basic nursing care. It was approaching 5 a.m. when Wahiba and her son were safely installed in the 'female medical' grass hut of the hospital compound. Rachida and I drew up a care plan which we explained to the family carers. We kept the suspected diagnosis to ourselves until our team doctor Ann carried out her clinical examination later that morning. Deep in my heart I knew we were only postponing the bad news.

As dawn broke and the sun's rising marked the start of another new day, Rachida and I drank a glass of tea in the *souk* (camp market). We spent some time sharing the joys and pains of our work as midwives, recognizing once again the huge weight of responsibility the life of the mother and her unborn baby placed on us. 'You know, Lizzy, I think it would be wiser not to tell Wahiba's family the seriousness of her condition,' came Rachida's remark after some time of reflective silence. 'It's not that I'm afraid of being blamed for the outcome of her delivery; it's just that I feel you would be crushing their hope of sustained life. They desperately need that hope in order to be able to care for Wahiba.'

And care Wahiba's family did over the following days as she continued to remain semiconscious with a generalized right-sided paralysis of her whole body. My concern focused increasingly on her son who seemed to cry incessantly. It didn't take much to discover hunger as the root cause. Refusal of the lactating female members of the family to 'wet nurse' him struck me as rather unusual. I strongly encouraged the family to allow the baby to breast feed from his mother assuring them it would do Wahiba no harm and might even stimulate her to regain consciousness. My reasoning and request seemed to come up against a psychological brick wall of protection now building up around Wahiba. My feelings of frustration and helplessness mounted as sugary, unboiled, contaminated water was fed to the child from a communal feeding cup and spoon. 'That should satisfy him for a while!' exclaimed Wahiba's sister. I was now totally confused in my understanding of their hope of sustained life. Maybe such a hope extended only to Wahiba and not to her son. Maybe living a life of survival as refugees caused them to prioritize the life of the mother. Maybe the poor little fellow was being blamed for Wahiba's poor health. Maybe, maybe, maybe . . .

Day four after delivery found me despairing over a dehydrated, neglected child with acute diarrhoea. As oral rehydration therapy was commenced my heart remained heavy and once again confused. Balancing the little scrap on my feet while pouring warm water over his red raw bottom, I searched desperately with tears to determine what I could do for this child. My thoughts were drawn to the statement '*A healthy child is a picture of God, a hurting child of his Son.*'

This child had been so healthy and perfect when he entered the world at birth. The touch of a wonderful Creator was reflected in the perfection of his little body. Every last detail of his five fingers and five toes radiated that perfection. He had been 'fearfully and wonderfully made', created in the image of God. But in just these four days of his earthly life that health and perfection had became scarred by the infliction of pain and suffering. In his hunger pains, abdominal discomfort from a running bowel, and raw skin from the burning acid of diarrhoea, were reflected the pain and suffering of his Creator's Son. This was now a hurting child.

My humanity and caring instinct longed to take him home and care for him ourselves. We could buy goats' milk which was the next best to breast milk available. We could even use the condemned feeding bottle in the safe environment of good hygiene and boiled water. He would surely thrive and grow over

these early months of his life ... But what then? The sober question faced me with cold reality. My dreams carried him home to my mum in Ireland whom I fondly referred to as – 'the woman who lived in a shoe who had so many children she didn't know what to do!' My mum 'collected' hurting children so I knew she would welcome him with open arms. But, in my heart, I also knew it was only a dream: I had no right to remove this little one from his refugee environment when my contract came to a close in six months' time. It was difficult enough to gain permission for a refugee to leave the camp for treatment in the nearest Sudanese hospital! The paperwork of exit visas etc. for us as Westerners was already fraught with 'red tape' and invitations to bribery. This child could not slip out of the country in my hand luggage. So what would become of him then? I studied his wizened, worried little face, which now resembled that of an old man. His small hands were clenched in a fist and drawn close to his chest, his little knees drawn tight up to his abdomen in a longing to return to the foetal position in his mother's womb. How I longed for him to make that return to a place of refuge and security.

As I held Wahiba's little son, longing to make everything right for him, I recalled the story of a refugee child who was taken in by a German midwife working for a secular relief agency. Her team was one of the first to move into camp and provided much needed curative health care in the early days of emergency relief. One day an abandoned, malnourished, neglected baby was presented to Helga in the course of her work. Her response as an 'all powerful', 'all prestigious' Westerner was studied with interest by those around her. If the health and wealth of our developed world held the answers to all the rest of the world's problems, surely the plight of an abandoned baby was routine trivia! With relief aid at our fingertips, authority to give life-sustaining food for malnourished children and medical resources to combat life-threatening illnesses, we had the power and means to react in every situation. So Helga reacted by taking the baby into the safe haven of her team's compound. As a team they cared for 'Ben', employing an Eritrean girl to cover their daytime workhours and Ben's night feeds. He became the source of much joy, responding to good care and lots of attention. Helga felt fulfilled in her mission to save the lives of starving refugees. This child would surely have died if she hadn't cared!

The first six months of emergency relief aid passed quickly, perhaps too quickly for Ben. It was now time for Helga's organization to move on to the next disaster area with their crisis aid. The Eritrean maid was entrusted with Ben's ongoing care, her salary paid for a further six months. Infant feeding formula shipped in from Germany, a good supply of feeding bottles and piles of disposable nappies were handed over with Ben on the day marking the accomplishment of the team's mission. But Ben's Western clothes, nappies and feeding bottles didn't belong to the surrounding Eritrean refugee culture. He had become a symbol of the health and wealth of 'the West' losing identity with his own people. The muddy brown drinking water from the nearby lake soon clogged up the teat of his feeding bottle and made the infant formula go lumpy. The disposable nappies were unable to contain the ensuing diarrhoea and his Western sleep-suits were soon discarded as unpractical.

We could find no trace of Ben on our arrival in camp only weeks after Helga's departure. Our best community contacts failed to come up with any lead as to his whereabouts. With time's passing the mysterious silence told its own story. What Ben had become during his months of Western living was unsustainable in his return to refugee life. The hope of sustained life was lost in the face of a feeding bottle which stood as a death sentence in such an environment.

And now the hurting child lying in my arms pierced my innermost being. I could see in him the 'hurting child' of God's Son in the face of this world, a world which was the source of so much pain and suffering. I knew my Western health, wealth and power were insufficient in mounting a feeble effort to cut across this situation. Not all of them put together could buy the life of this child before me, a child belonging to a family who now held the responsibility for determining his future.

My response to the situation was being studied with interest by those around me. What could I offer? I now had a burning desire to communicate to these hurting refugees my Christian understanding of a suffering God – a God who weeps with them in their sorrow over Wahiba's illness, a God who feels their pain of separation and loss as refugees, a God who knows their battered human resources are insufficient to care for mother and baby, a God who understands the pain of having to making such a choice, a God ready to carry them when they can walk no more in the face of this earth's suffering, a God who holds this hurting child in the palm of his hand washing him with his tears. There was something very beautiful in the depths of its reality and experience, yet something very difficult for this Muslim family to comprehend with their concept of an all-powerful Allah who is totally detached from their pain and suffering.

The suffering of this child stood as a striking symbol of the God I knew and believed in, a God in whom their only hope of life lay! 'A hurting child – a picture of God's Son' now pointing to him in whom lay the key to that hope, a hope expressed through that Son's suffering and death. I now committed this child's life and suffering into his care.

On my routine morning visit to the hospital on my last day 'on call' in camp, I immediately noted the marked absence of Wahiba's son. My eyes quickly scanned the corner of the hospital building where Wahiba still lay motionless. No baby! To my enquiry about the child Wahiba's sister's honest, matter of fact remark cut through me, – 'When Wahiba is well again she can have another baby. If by any chance she doesn't get better she won't be needing the child anyway.' A surge of questions rose within me as I fought back my emotions. If only I had gone against Rachida's advice and told the family that their hope of sustained earthly life lay in the child and not Wahiba . . . If only, if only, if only . . .

Once again I was hit by a deep sense of failure. Its flowing from an even deeper sense of helplessness lay in my inability to understand and respond fully to the deep needs of these people. I could picture the tiny cold limp body wrapped in a piece of white cloth being carried out by the menfolk into the desert for burial, under cover of the previous night. The hope of new life received at delivery might be women's business but the hope of a better life to come in the 'laying to rest' of those who had departed from this world, was men's business.

At six o'clock that evening as the sun dropped out of the sky once again I handed over the responsibility of the labouring women in camp to our team's doctor as she started her week 'on call'. Climbing into the Landrover that would carry me back to the town where we lived, I longed for my much loved bed and an undisturbed night's sleep. My body was once again tired and my emotions completely drained.

Night had fallen as we headed for home. Leaving camp my eyes were drawn to the wasteland into which the sun had sunk only an hour previously. My thoughts wandered back over the 'growing' experiences of the previous week. There had been plenty more new lives (in the face of death) to hope in and sustained lives to be thankful for, all interwoven with the unquenchable hope of a better life to come.

Passing a procession of white-dressed male folk carrying the form of a body wrapped in white cloth, I scanned their faces in empathy with their difficult task. As if in silent acknowledgement one of the men turned toward me and caught my eye. A cold shiver went through me as I immediately recognized him as Wahiba's brother. His silent gaze told all. Mother and son were now to be reunited . . . this time in a grave which lay far on the horizon in the direction of their longed-for homeland. Reunited only seven days after physical birth had driven a cruel wedge of suffering into their once-shared special bond.

I wondered if Wahiba's family would ever live to regret the unnecessary 'slipping away' of a healthy child who had had all to live for. Their pursuit of hope in sustained life had been so strong. Tonight they would be hoping even more for a better life to come. Their burning tear-filled eyes would scan the horizon until dawn, when the sun's rising *would* bring renewed hope once again.

# 6

# All Sunshine Makes a Desert

Dawn was breaking in eastern Sudan as I set out on foot from our 'on call' compound towards the refugee camp. Situated a couple of kilometres away from camp beside the only local source of water, the compound sat amidst a cluster of shade-giving thorn bushes. Unfortunately we were not the only ones attracted to this pleasant haven of moisture and vegetation. It was obviously the location of choice for all the female mosquitoes in the region to give birth to their young. Thankfully our daytime living could pass swiftly under the protection of a mosquito net in time for their mainly nocturnal activities. Nevertheless, the 'twilight zone' seemed to provide them with enough of our pulsating blood to procreate. Such was the harmony of our cohabitation.

The large brown muddy lake lying behind me as I walked was the product of a dammed river whose source lay high in the Eritrean mountains. The lake served not only as a life-sustaining source of water in this wasteland but also as a precious psychological link with home for the refugees. Its rippling waves brought news of their homeland. To its shores came a constant stream of semi-nomadic Sudanese tribesmen in search of water for their herds. During the stiflingly hot summer months they camped close to the water's edge, awaiting the cooler autumn days when wanderlust would draw them into the desert once again. This water had many uses: people washed their clothes and themselves in it; its refreshing drops were sought after to cool both overheated Landrover engines and tall dusty camels. Urinating people and animals added to its volume, as did the dead donkeys whose carcases were washed into its depths from the shores. With its 'chocolate milkshake' appearance it was pumped up to the refugee camp for drinking, where it became a dreaded source of infection and disease as well as a life-sustaining element.

I giggled inwardly as I remembered my own quest for refreshment in the early suffocatingly hot weeks that I had first spent in camp. Late one afternoon the cool lapping waters of the lake drew me to its shores inviting me to dip my body into its depths. The offer was tempting and the visible absence of any other human being encouraged me to take the plunge. Availing myself of this unique opportunity of complete privacy to strip off right down to my swimsuit, I folded my clothes neatly into a pile and placed them close to the shore. I soon discovered that the longing to plunge into the water with its reflecting waves was more appealing than the actual experience. The lake's 'depths' turned out to be *very* shallow and the ground under foot *very* muddy. It took a lot of slipping and sliding to get to a point where I could sit in a reasonable amount of watery mud. My thoughts were miles away from the water's edge because all my concentration went into keeping upright. Meanwhile unbeknown to me a herd of about thirty camels had emerged from the desert and were wading into the lake. The once-deserted shoreline behind me was now crowded by these huge animals pursuing their favourite pastime of slowly replenishing their water reserves. I realized I was in for a long haul so found myself a muddy heap to sit on and waited . . . By this time some local children had gathered and started snapping their arms together to warn me of crocodiles! I knew I had only one chance with a 'croc' but thought maybe I would have two chances with a camel! Hurriedly deciding to cut my losses I headed for the shore where three camels were by this time making an enjoyable meal of my cotton skirt and T-shirt. Their generosity had left me my flip-flops, as rubber obviously didn't agree with their delicate digestive systems. With the sun setting and goose pimples rising on my cold scummy body, the camel owner and I struck a bargain: he would clear a path for me to reach the shore if I gave him some medicine for one of his camels with an irritating cough that kept him awake at night! My parting comments made it very clear that I would be unavailable to treat certain camels that might suffer from constipation over the next couple of days!

As a result of that muddy and embarrassing incident, word of my midwifery skills was passed around the semi-nomadic community represented by that one man and his camels. As I walked into work that morning my eyes were drawn to the waste expanse which they called home for ten months of the year. It stood in such contrast to life at the water's edge yet drew like a magnet those whose lives were marked by wanderlust. It was a hard life to be born into . . . wind-blown, sun-scorched faces telling many a sad or painful story. The rising sun baking the sand which now slipped through my toes as I walked, was the same sun which scorched and hardened these people's faces. It was also the element which had wiped out all trace of plant life from this expanse of sandy dirt. *All* sunshine had made this place a desert!

On my arrival at work that morning a shy, veiled Sudanese girl awaited me. Her appearance was characteristic of a nomadic people often viewed on camel back striding into the setting sun. I was immediately impressed by the beauty of lavish black curls bursting from under her veil and sitting like a canopy above her dark eyes outlined with charcoal. From just below the bridge of her nose another long veil, this one embroidered with silver beads, fell like a bib to her chest. A treasured wedding gift from her husband it ensured that even her smile was now his private property. All eating and drinking in public was carried out discreetly behind this long veil which struck me as suffocating in the summer heat. It never ceased to amaze me how much could be communicated to the world through the small 'attic' window these women were permitted. Yet I always saw their eyes as bay windows to their hearts where so much of life's joy, pain and sorrow waited to be shared. The intensity of a single gaze held the potential to tell all. Veiling of the body took the form of layers of traditional flowing black material with brightly coloured pieces of appliqued cotton. I found the traditional dress of these tribes-women very striking.

Malika's young eyes were pregnant with pain and sadness. My knowing that it took a great deal of courage for her to seek me out prepared the way for what she was about to share. At the age of thirteen she had found herself a child-bride married to her thirty-five-year-old first cousin. Even before the onset of her menstrual flow, a knife was used to open up the anterior scar of the radical female circumcision she had undergone at the age of six. This scar guaranteed virginity at wedlock and only with surgical opening was it possible for her husband to consummate their marriage. Further opening was later required to allow passage of each baby at delivery. Re-suturing of the enlarged orifice was always sought afterwards for the ongoing satisfaction of her husband. Such trauma in these tribeswomen's lives was accepted as their 'lot' but the pain Malika was now sharing was unacceptable. Ten years of married life had blessed her with four pregnancies which brought her joy and fulfilment as a woman. But each time these nine months of longing and waiting had ended in the delivery of a dead baby. No one was able to tell her the cause of the deaths which had put her marriage under serious threat. The tribe's traditional birth-attendant refused to have anything more to do with Malika for fear her misfortune would be attributed to the birth-attendant's power to cast the 'evil eye' (evil spells). Women like the wise birth-attendant were known to possess special power to cast such spells through an eye of envy, willing misfortune. Maybe someone possessing such power had cast an eye of envy on Malika when she had married such a handsome man at such a young age! There were many jealous tribeswomen known to her who longed for her husband as their own. Whatever the motive behind the misfortune apparently inflicted on her, the desired effect of destroying her marriage was evident.

So it was that in the fourth month of her fifth pregnancy Malika came to me requesting my care through to delivery. Compassion for this girl gripped me as I personally committed myself to her well-being and that of her baby. I felt confident that my more advanced professional training would equip me to see her through this delivery, knowing only too well the limited experience of local midwives when it came to handling complications. I could detect a ray of hope breaking through Malika's now smiling eyes as she slipped out of the door with promises to return at two-weekly intervals throughout her pregnancy. She left me feeling very privileged at the depth of trust she had displayed in sharing her story. I knew something special was in store for us.

The weeks of Malika's pregnancy passed quickly, marked by her faithful and regular appearance in the refugee camp for check-ups. Every two weeks she would arrive with the rising sun and wait patiently for my undivided attention. With her shy disposition she needed the moral support and security offered by the two older women who always accompanied her. At midday her husband would return to carry them back across the desert by camel. These hours of waiting presented many opportunities for health education as well as creating avenues down which a greater understanding of Malika's cultural background could be gained. Her baby was growing, developing and moving inside her ever-enlarging womb. A strong heartbeat was detected early on in the sixth month and on examination all seemed well for both mother and unborn child. I relaxed into the normality of the proceedings feeling reassured that all would be well this time.

By the ninth month of pregnancy Malika felt secure and comfortable enough to expose her abdomen for examination. Up to this point I had only been permitted to do my routine checks of her developing baby through the layers of black cotton which covered her whole body. During one forgetful moment while drinking, she even gave me a glimpse of the smile that lay behind her silver-beaded veil. Such was the depth of the growing trust communicated from her unveiling heart to mine through her dark eyes. Anticipation of delivery gripped both of us. Final preparations to welcome this precious child into the world were in the making. Malika put together a little bundle of clean pieces of cloth with a bar of soap while I made doubly sure my back-up necessities for complications (should they arise) were ready.

I flopped exhausted onto my bed in our 'on call' compound one sticky Saturday afternoon. A long, busy, dusty day was coming to a close and a rapidly developing sore throat was beginning to

claim my voice. Any hopes of rest were soon shattered by the arrival of a camel which stuck its head over the fence of our enclosure. I recognized it as the one whose irritating cough I had been asked to treat months previously. 'What could be wrong with him now?' I asked myself while scanning its apparently fit and healthy face. My thoughts were soon redirected as the camel's rider had come charged with a very important message: Malika was in labour and awaiting my arrival at the hospital building in camp. There was no time to lose as I collected together all I would need for the next few hours.

Physically low resources started responding nicely to the surge of adrenaline in my bloodstream as did clarity of thinking and judgement. Yet snatched moments of apprehension were enough to remind me of my complete dependence on divine wisdom and strength in the task before me.

On arrival at the hospital building I found Malika in the early stages of labour. As promised she had come immediately the pains of childbirth had caught her attention. My desire to monitor closely both mother and unborn baby from early on could now be fulfilled. On examination all appeared well so we relaxed into a routine of waiting and assessing progress. The contractions gained momentum, the baby edged its way further down the birth canal, and the world lingered in anticipation as the moment of delivery drew nearer.

At sunset the grass building in which we were housed became reliant on a paraffin wick for light. All corners of the hut were now shrouded in the dark shadows of night. From within these shadows came unexpected visitors. A frog hopped its way across the cement floor as Malika bravely rode each labour pain in silent dignity and acceptance. The frog was soon followed by a hungry cat which couldn't quite get its paw around the unpredictable hopping. After a chase the frog squeezed neatly under the narrow gap between the grass wall and cement floor leaving a disgusted cat frustrated by its inability to follow. This veil of protection between the frog and the cat drew my thinking back to Malika. I could sense the psychological protection and support her continually veiled face gave her in the masking of her pain – yet in reality her eyes disclosed all. My own eyes filled with tears of compassion and admiration as I observed this girl's incredible strength and self-control in action. There was a richness to her life that I found myself drawn to. Our meeting eyes became a deep source of shared encouragement as the pains of childbirth intensified and my ailing throat reduced my voice to a whisper. In the evening silence a large scorpion emerged from the shadows unperturbed by the ebbing of Malika's breathing pattern in response to each pain. The cat scarpered and our stinging friend took his leave through the same gap the frog had used.

It was approaching midnight when Malika's baby seemed close to making its grand entry into the world. Regular monitoring of the heartbeat had revealed nothing abnormal up to this point, so I had allowed nature to take its course in determining the progress of labour. Horror struck like a thunderbolt when, quite unexpectedly, that rhythmic pulsation suddenly dropped. Nausea surged over me: I realised something was going drastically wrong. Wasting no time I quickly pulled out my hand-pump-operated vacuum-extractor, applying it briskly to the baby's head. Six to seven long minutes of pumping were required to allow the application cup to create the necessary suction before any pulling could take place to speed up delivery. My hoarse voice forced an urgent whisper pleading with Malika to push as I pulled. The panic on my face could not be veiled. Thump . . . thump . . . thump . . . the baby's heartbeat reduced even further as the application cup lost its suction and sent me flying backwards against the grass wall of the hut.

Tears of desperation and frustration were now pouring down my face. Thump . . . thump . . . thump . . . thump . . . as six more precious minutes of emotional and professional agony were lived through in re-siting the application cup. 'Please God, don't let me lose this baby,' I pleaded desperately as I listened in total disbelief to life slipping away before me. An arm in muscular spasm from all the pumping now pulled with all its might in a last effort to get this child delivered quickly while there was still hope. Thump . . . .

The head descended in a matter of minutes – delivering into my trembling hands a fresh stillbirth. Frantic efforts to instil life-giving breath into the baby's lungs and massage her heart back into action were fruitless. Shock, unbelief and devastation joined together in a whirlpool of emotion as I held the warm yet lifeless body of a fully developed baby girl. Her dark brown eyes and mop of jet black hair were unmistakably those of her mother. Like a child I found myself pleading with her to breathe in the life-giving air all around her. 'Oh little one, please don't do this to me; your mummy needs you *so* much! *Please, please, please, please*, don't do this to us! Oh God, NO!' For the first time in my life I was sounding the profound depths of silence.

When all seemed lost I ran into the dark shadows of the night air for protection and veiling of my emotions, totally incapable of looking Malika in the face as failure hit me like a ton of bricks. I was professionally and emotionally devastated. My Western midwifery training had not prepared me for such situations. No baby had ever died on me like this before. I had come to Sudan armed with confidence in my life-preserving skills and high standard of care, equipped with all the knowledge and training necessary to stand between the cradle and the grave . . . or so I had thought! How then could this life have slipped so freely out of my hands? In the light of a half moon I sat beside the main water pump and sobbed . . . 'What must Malika think of me?' The brilliance of the moon reflected in the pool of water at my feet invited my attention. I wanted to cry out to the heavens above but even my strained whisper had now left me. My tears acknowledged my broken-hearted failure before the Creator of the starry heavens. He alone could give me the strength and ability to face myself and Malika.

With a deep breath I pulled myself together and returned to where she lay cradling her baby daughter. Those dark tear-filled eyes engaged with mine as I tried to force enough air through my vocal cords to sound the word 'Sorry'. I felt wretched to the depths of my devastated being and 'sorry' seemed a pathetic expression of that state. Nothing could have prepared me for what came next. Slowly she removed her veil and we stood emotionally naked before each other. With the full radiance of her face she expressed her heartfelt thanks for all I had done. Knowing I had offered my best she felt so grateful to be at the receiving end of my care. As for her lifeless daughter . . . 'Allah Raghlab'! – God alone is the victor! Acceptance was all that was asked of her to live another day. This day marked not only the death of her daughter but the certain death of her marriage – 'Allah Raghlab'! Her unveiled face reflected the depth of her indebtedness to me and there was no mistaking the sincerity of her words. This unexpected showering with such a fountain of gratitude dissolved my inner being even further.

At sunset the following day Malika mounted a camel in dignity and headed for home. The skies were pregnant with the dark clouds that marked the beginning of the rainy season. A soft drizzle washed my face as I watched the silhouette of camel and rider reduce to a dot on the horizon and eventually disappear. I knew it was a final parting as these rains marked the start of ten months of desert wanderings for her people. Yet our final embrace (with reveiled faces) affirmed the place in our unveiled hearts that would always be there for each other and the time we had shared. For me it would take time and tears to untangle the emotions and feelings resulting from my encounter with Malika. But maybe one day I would discover what it was that had touched my heart in such a profound way through this meeting. A clap of thunder finally broke my gaze, warning me of an imminent downpour.

Over the next days rain washed the sun-scorched ground I had only ever known as lifeless, dry and baked. The familiar bleak landscape became a painting marked by the hand of an artist who swept his brush, dipped in green paint, across this tract of desert. Sun and rain joined together in turning the barren ground into an unbelievable blossoming garden. New life burst from every pore. The imagery struck me hard as my thoughts were still far on the horizon with Malika. Often I had reflected on the unrelenting sunshine that had made this desert. How easy it was always to seek sunshine in my life – the sunshine of love, success, joy, achievement, peace and giving, the sunshine of being all things to all people in a desire to show them the depth of my caring and that of the God who cares for me. But failure, weakness, inade-quacy, emotional and professional devastation, heart-rending pain, suffering, loss, grief and profound weeping didn't feature on that agenda. Instead they appeared as the threatening black clouds now clapping with thunder, ignited with lightning, and bursting with rain, threatening to destruct, destroy and devastate. Yet if they were accepted, yielded to, and lived through, a blossoming garden would be mine. A rich garden of deep empathy for these people, an understanding of their suffering, a Christ-like compassion radiating from my unveiled face, a God-given love to minister healing to their hurting lives, and an overwhelming joy as we delighted together in that healing.

The jewel of my encounter with Malika now became clearer. Her life had always been lived between intense sunshine and merciless rain. Her ingrained attitude of acceptance allowed the two to work together in cultivating a blossoming garden, a garden that could be viewed through the bay window of her heart, or more strikingly in the radiance of the face behind the veil.

# 7

# A Kaleidoscope of Colour
# . . . weaving Life's Tapestry

At ten to five one Friday in June, on the eve of a bank holiday weekend, the phone rang in my family home in Dublin. Ruth, the social worker responsible for the foster children we welcomed, wanted to speak to Mum . . .

'Hello Margaret, it's Ruth here, needing some of your pearls of wisdom as we're in a bit of a quandary'. Such an introduction usually meant there was a child who needed sorting out. Mum braced herself and encouraged Ruth to continue. 'You see, Margaret, today we were landed with a rather traumatized American teenager whose parents are probably at this moment actually touching down in the States.' Mum's face registered bewilderment as she asked why the child wasn't landing on the other side of the Atlantic with them. 'Did she miss her flight or something?' The ensuing silence was finally broken by, 'Unfortunately, Margaret, it's the "or something" – her parents deliberately left her behind. She has now become our responsibility and was handed over to us classified as a "hopeless case". It's a long story and I'll fill you in on all the details when I see you but basically we all reckon if you can't do something with this child, nobody can! It's a desperate situation.'

No more needed to be said. A room was quickly cleared, a bed made up and a small vase of red roses placed on the dressing table. Just as the commercial world was closing down for the long weekend, we welcomed a lost and bewildered Anna into our home.

Anna was one hundred per cent American, having grown up in Arkansas. Her natural parents, who were alcoholics, struggled to raise two small children within the context of their addiction and marital difficulties. So, at the age of five, Anna and her three-year-old sister Beth were signed over for adoption. These already traumatized children were adopted by another American couple who later divorced. The adoptive mother was awarded custody of the children and took them with her into two subsequent marriages. The children's needs deepened as the trauma of their early years failed to be worked through in a stable experience of healing family life. The rejection process was augmented as blame for the failure of these marriages fell on the children's shoulders. It was a heavy load for such young children to carry – for Anna in particular. Her cry for help manifested itself in behavioural problems. 'Please, please take notice of me – I'm hurting *so* much.' This pitiful cry was met with further rejection, plus physical and emotional abuse. As inability to handle this child led to frustration and despair, professional help was sought. A prescription for strong medication, tranquillizers and sedatives, was justified on the grounds of psychiatric ill health – after all that was the only possible explanation for her intolerable behaviour! So Anna progressed from being an unmanageable alert teenager to becoming an unmanageable sedated teenager. A decision to dump her on the Irish health services was then taken. The end of a short work contract in Dublin for her stepfather provided the perfect opportunity to be rid of this problem child and return to life as 'normal' in the States with Beth (the quieter and preferred daughter of the two).

And so thirteen-year-old Anna . . . deeply traumatized and doped to the eyeballs, came to share in our family life. She was to bring with her into our home an erupting kaleidoscope of colour . . . coloured threads in the weaving of life's rich tapestry.

**Black – the pit of shock, lostness and despair.**

The black thread was introduced into our home that Friday evening. This hurting teenager came shrouded in a near-tangible blanket of abuse, hurt and rejection. She was solemn and withdrawn muttering only such words as were essential to communicate her basic needs. Shock and disbelief cushioned her from the reality of where she now found herself. Survival became the name of the game, and she withdrew even further to fight alone. Not the slightest hint of a crevice in a dark shell of protection yielded to an outpouring of our loving care and concern. We were in for a time of it: this would be a hard nut to crack.

Those early days in particular were marked by Anna's tormented spirit venting itself in outbursts of incredible rage and anger, all exacerbated by the process of weaning her off the unnecessary medication. Doors slamming, displacement of furniture, and books orbiting all became part of the daily drama. These episodes were punctuated by sleep and periods of time spent staring through glazed eyes at the fragrant red roses adorning the dressing table. Though we did not know it at the time, those roses, freshly picked from the garden, were an essential link for Anna with the Creator of the universe. Despite her perceiving God as watching from a distance, the simplicity and beauty of these flowers somehow communicated his presence to Anna in a way nothing else could.

As the summer passed and the detoxification process continued, reality had to be faced. The tip of the iceberg was uncovered and the pain was woeful. God did not remain at a distance: his near-tangible presence in our family home enabled us to survive during those traumatic days, weeks and months. The days were long, nights cut short, patience stretched to its limits, and refills of love frequently requested. Yet within the blur of survival, a reassuring faith helped us to believe that all this black had the potential to be a striking background for one of life's most beautiful tapestries. It was a faith that made us 'hang in there' . . . in anticipation!

**Red – Raw open wounds of hurt and rejection; the colour of pain and love.**

Autumn's passing to winter brought with it the colour red glimpsed here and there through holes now appearing in the black blanket of protection. None of us had ever lived before in close proximity to such a shocking, hurting product of our world. The pain of rejection, double, triple, quadruple rejection. The pain of separation . . . lived every day of Anna's conscious existence. The pain of abuse – physical, emotional and spiritual, piling up like burning coals over the years of desperate crying for help. The pain of misunderstanding and being misunderstood. The pain of failure. The pain of a lost identity. The pain of major emotional wounds.

And those red roses – a symbol of such beauty with the potential to inflict so much pain if not handled with care. Red roses that would become for us a painful symbol of love as we shared in the trauma of Anna's life and sought to carry her along the road to healing.

**Blue – A yearning need for bonding – to be loved and to love.**

As we approached the first anniversary of Anna's arrival *chez nous*, we spent a family weekend with friends in the country. These days away immersed in nature brought summer to the door of our hearts. We had lived through the long dark cold days of winter and spring had brought with it the promise of new life bursting out of that bleak time. Long walks across fields, through hedges and over gates opened our eyes and ears to all the evidence of spring around: lambs learning to walk on wobbly legs, pools full of swimming tadpoles fast developing into frogs, baby birds hatching from the security of their incubating shells, and trees laden with blossom as new leaves unfurled. During this time of 'drinking in' the beauty of the countryside and creation in all its glory, Anna discovered a helplessly squawking casualty fallen from its nest. Stooping, she gently picked up the feathery little creature, cupping him in the security of her hands. With tender strokes her finger calmed his restlessness, bringing peace. Compassion poured from her eyes with promises of shelter, love and healing. The little hurting bird seemed to yield to this outpouring of love and care. During those brief moments of encounter, to our amazement he became the channel through which Anna was finally released to identify her own brokenness and needs. Through the frailty of this created, wounded being, Anna found expression of her own frailty and need for shelter, love and healing. Her tear-filled eyes radiated deep longing as she finally set out on the road to healing.

**Colourless Lemonade**

On the wall in our kitchen is a poster which wisely advises :

WHEN LIFE GIVES YOU LEMONS MAKE LEMONADE!

As our lives became closely interwoven with Anna's, there was no problem identifying the 'lemons' of family living – lemons with the capacity to make wonderful lemonade! Anna's unfolding vivacious personality and rich American cultural conditioning helped us to enjoy the 'lemonade' side of life. At crucial moments her loud American accent could rise high above our soft Dublin ones. If you wanted to be heard in our house you had to speak with a loud deep southern Texan accent! Our family's healthy eating policy was seroiusly undermined as peanut-butter and jelly sandwiches became an integral part of breakfast, supper and snacks – as did banana milkshakes and chocolate chip muffins. Ugh! A visit to McDonalds was now a monthly special followed by an ice cream from Baskin Robbins. Not great for the waistline – or the family budget – yet Mum's wisdom recognized these as important links with the land of 'stars and stripes'. Anna's decidedly 'off' days (i.e. more off than usual) accompanying a woman's hormonal rollercoaster, were fondly referred to as the 'Moody monthly'. I often wondered how the publishers of such a famous American Christian magazine would take to being associated with period pains! Trash cans, trunks and hoods replaced bins, boots and bonnets as we became more American by the day.

When we celebrated our second Christmas with Anna, I remember being landed with the 'privilege' of taking her shopping with our two younger sisters, Rebekah and Jane. It was Christmas Eve and sibling disharmony and discontent were not helped by the push and shove of last minute panic-shoppers. We took refuge in an overcrowded McDonalds, propping ourselves up against the wall to eat our burgers and french fries. By this stage all communication between the girls had ceased thanks to a final 'bust up' over an imbalance in money spent on each other's Christmas presents. Sulking added to the already tense silence as the world continued to buzz by. My attention wandering, I scanned the faces of the other suffering shoppers; my eyes came to rest on a highly pregnant woman standing in the long queue for orders. Two small children swung from her skirt beneath the bursting shopping bags hanging from each shoulder. My heart went out to this young mum weighed down by the heat and hassle of the day. As if in response to my sympathetic thoughts, her knees suddenly went from under her and she fainted into the arms of the unassuming man standing right behind! His order was for three big Macs, five large french fries, four chocolate milkshakes and one diet coke . . . with no mention of one very pregnant woman, two children and forty shopping bags!

Holding on to her in a state of confusion and shock he continued to mumble his list of orders lest he forget it all. A reviving glass of water was brought and she was finally propped up on a chair and fanned with an empty chicken nuggets carton retrieved from the bin. The silence in our small group of four was finally broken as all eyes were riveted on the drama. 'What's wrong with that lady Lizzy, is she sick or something?' was Jane's concerned question. Anna never missed an opportunity to have the last word so her reply came fast and furious – 'Would you ever get a grip, Jane! Can't you see, you idiot, she's having contraptions!' Thankfully my more informed medical judgment assured me it was a simple faint and not an imminent delivery in the middle of McD's. The stress of the day was suddenly defused as I dissolved into laughter. The 'contraptions' of labouring with life's lemons sure produced some fun lemonade! To this day (and two deliveries later) Jane still can't remember if labour pains are contraptions or contractions – all thanks to that memorable Christmas Eve in McDonalds.

## White – The colour of purity.

Anna's need for shelter, love and security drew her closer into the heart of our family as well as into the warmth of our local church. The loving care of this Christian community – our extended family – accepted and embraced Anna in a tangible way. Her growing appreciation of the true character of God as she experienced it through the working out of my parents' faith, was reinforced by the lives of these people. She was beginning to sound the depths of divine healing love.

Anna built up a special relationship with our rector, Paul, who weathered the storm of her frequent barrage of questions and outbursts of anger towards God. Through his patient listening and careful handling, Anna's tormented spirit found more peace. A desire to trust the God of that secure love and peace became evident.

The autumn of Anna's fifteenth birthday brought with it a desire to attend confirmation classes with a view to making a personal affirmation of the vows taken on her behalf at her christening as a baby. A date was scheduled for the spring. During one of these classes Anna was asked how she knew who God was. Her response was as sincere as it was striking: 'How do I know who God is? Gee, I know who he is because of the Wilsons!'

Early spring brought with it again the first signs of new life bursting forth from the still icy cold winter ground. It never ceases to amaze me that crocuses and snowdrops brave the harsh ice to blossom in all their beauty – I would have thought it would be less painful to wait for a warmer patch of weather! Yet those little snowdrops and crocuses stand as a symbol of a beauty forced out by the freezing cold – a beauty displayed against a bleak background unique to that harsh time of year. In some similar way the nipping frost of life's trials and afflictions started to force out an incredible beauty in Anna. Like the snowdrops and crocuses she seemed to bear witness to the purifying power behind the sharp, piercing frost with its ability to promote revival, budding and blossoming. As the nipping frost of loss and rejection, the icy sting of pain and separation, and the numb chill of heartache were yielded to divine healing love, the beauty of a pure God-given deep joy and peace blossomed in her life.

### Yellow – The warm rays of human love, friendship and relationships.

Once Anna had opened herself up to be loved she uncovered her own amazing capacity to love. She made many friends through her school years, though like money they were often easier in the making than in the keeping!

Trust in friendships was often destroyed by the wavering commitment of others. Anna's mature insight into the importance of human friendship was not shared by everyone. All the additional hurt only made her more determined to make some sense of human relationships as the struggle to be loved and to love continued. More often than not she found herself drawn to those who lived similar hurting lives – after all their shared experience gave birth to an understanding of life akin to her own. Yet a conflict continued to rage between this craving to be loved and a fear of being hurt again. Like someone learning to windsurf, time and time again she rebalanced herself on that board, slowly and tediously re-erected the sail, set it to the wind, enjoyed the elation of a few moments of journeying only to lose balance and topple over again . . . hitting the water with an even greater splash.

Shortly after her sixteenth birthday a special friendship developed with Carl, who soon responded to Anna's increasing expression of warmth and love. Red roses became the symbol of his growing love for her, roses delivered on the day of her school Debutantes ball, on the morning of her seventeenth birthday, and on Valentine's day. Such was her love for Carl that she had a blossoming red rose tattooed onto her left upper arm. She had fallen hard for this guy! Anna's infectious laughter became more and more part of daily life as she relaxed into the relative security of this relationship and enjoyed the social life of a seventeen year old.

But teenage romances can often be short and intense – and so this one unfortunately proved to be. Carl was obviously not ready to commit himself to working with the complexities of Anna's background, so opted out of their relationship in pursuit of a less complicated 'catch'. This disappointment was painfully hard to take. The endless tearful days, nursing a broken heart were lived under the security of a comforting duvet and listening to Bette Midler's *From a distance*:

> *From a distance there is harmony and it echoes through the land. It's the hope of hopes, it's the love of loves, it's the heart of every man.*[1]

Anna's quest for harmonious love continued.

---

[1] Copyright; Julie Gold Music Publishing. Permission sought.

**Purple – The richness of healing. To give and receive.**

Leaving school at seventeen put a big question mark over Anna's future career. As her true nature found space and encouragement to blossom, so it became evident that an empathy with, and love for, those who were hurting in this world was central in her heart. In particular she loved children. So it was with great excitement that we welcomed the news of a place to train as a nursery nurse. Anna felt released into a work she loved. At eighteen she qualified as a fully-fledged nursery nurse, choosing to work with disabled adults and children. She brought a ray of sunshine into the lives of society's hurting community and they loved her immensely.

**Green – The colour of life, the Emerald Isle, shamrocks, leprechauns and an Irish passport.**

With Anna's eighteenth birthday came the emotional turmoil of a big decision. Now deemed by law to be a fully responsible adult she was free to live her own life on either side of the Atlantic. She felt a strong pull back to the USA – the land of her roots and dreams. Maybe she could find her sister Beth again and all would be well. Yet choosing that option meant relinquishing her rights to Irish citizenship; there would be no turning back. She knew that it would also mean relinquishing her rights to a family – maybe the only one she had in the world. Yet the pull to greener pastures the other side of the Atlantic ocean became stronger as the dilemma continued.

It was during this time that an unexpected letter arrived via our local American embassy from Anna's natural mother in the States. News of the plight of her daughters had filtered through the 'jungle telephone' causing her much concern. Anna's 'dumping' in Ireland had been followed by Beth's 'kicking out' of home soon after returning to the States. She had taken to the streets and joined a band of Mexican travellers dealing in drugs. *Her* quest for love left her pregnant at fourteen and celebrating her fifteenth birthday with motherhood.

Renewed contact with her natural mother brought for Anna an ever-increasing hope that maybe this was the road of return to her yet – unfulfilled childhood dreams. Maybe now she could discover her true identity and all the pain and hurt of the past would be wiped away. It was a dream far removed from reality, and it left us fearful of the effects of even more shattered hopes. Five years of full immersion in healing family life and the painful untangling of life's traumatic experiences had brought about a transformation in this hopeless case. Yet the process of healing continued with much more still waiting to be dealt with.

A paralysing fear of making the wrong decision gripped Anna. Mum's wisdom proposed a compromise. She suggested a 'look-see', 'spying out the land', 'see how you feel' summer holiday back in the States with her natural mother and stepfather. It needed a lot of courage for Anna to take this step as moving out of her place of security revealed once again the depth of her emotional vulnerability. How we all longed to go with her to provide the love and support she so desperately cried out for! But we knew in our hearts that it was a journey she had to make alone.

During that six-week holiday Anna realized that her future no longer lay in the land of her childhood dreams. Although her time with her mother had been generally positive she seemed a complete stranger who could not offer Anna a base of healing family life. It proved a very lonely holiday when the reality of what was no more had to be faced and final cords cut. Anna started to count the days when a reunion with her real family in the Emerald Isle would be possible. Green *was* the colour of life – the renewed life she had experienced in that land and the life full of hope she had yet to live. 'I love you Mom and Dad, and can't wait to see you again' – such heartfelt words expressed from the other side of the Atlantic. And so she returned home.


**Black and Red – The pit of shock, pain and grief.**

One cold dark evening in February Anna left after supper to pay a surprise call on some friends. She would hire a video *en route* for them to watch together. Little did we know that her parting words, as she walked out of the front door, were to be her final farewell. For as we gathered around the television to watch the nine o'clock news, Anna came into direct collision with a car in the fast lane of the dual carriageway only five minutes walk from our house. There were no witnesses to the accident and no form of identification could be found on her person. As we settled down for the night at 11.30 p.m. surgeons were fighting to save Anna's life in our nearest referral hospital. As midnight approached Mum became concerned, as Anna hadn't phoned to say she would be late. At nineteen she wanted to take full responsibility for her life yet she deeply respected the concern of others. Maybe the video had gone on longer than expected and the passing of time had slipped her attention. Mum and Dad dozed, awaiting the familiar sound of Anna's key in the door, before turning off the bedside light and giving way to a more profound slumber. At 2 a.m. as the surgeons lost the four hour fight to save Anna's life, Mum sat bolt upright in bed with a start. Something deep within sent an electric shock through her body, a shock of warning, a warning that something was drastically wrong . . .

The black pit of shock, pain and grief was indescribable. A squad car arrived at our front door within minutes of a telephone inquiry to our local police station. With minimal explanation they whisked Mum off to our local hospital where the horrors of the tragedy unfolded like an unimaginable nightmare. It was a painfully brutal end to a life that had already experienced so much of life's cruelty – a mutilated faceless body identifiable only by the tattooed rose that remained intact on the upper arm. A rose that now became the only way of confirming with deep piercing pain that this was indeed our beloved Anna.

**Gold – For a throne! Golden fields of ripened wheat.**

On the day of Anna's funeral, each member of our family carried a single red rose and placed it on her coffin. Those roses were a symbol of deep love, our love that went with her into the grave and beyond, beyond to where in her new life of complete healing and freedom, she danced through golden fields of ripened wheat. Such was the glimpse of what lies beyond that God gave Mum as we wept our goodbyes.

> *For what is it to die than to stand naked in the wind and melt into the sun? And what is it to cease breathing but to free the breath from its restless tides, that it may rise and expand and seek God unencumbered? Only when you drink from the river of silence shall you indeed sing. And when you have reached the mountain top then you shall begin to climb. And when the earth shall claim your limbs, then shall you truly dance.*
>
> Kahlil Gibran.[2]

For Anna that freedom truly to dance could not be experienced until the earth had claimed her limbs and freed her to behold the brilliant colour of gold . . . the throne of a God waiting to embrace her with complete healing. Her final destination had now been reached and *Gee* was she dancing!

But what of us left behind? The colours of black and red would be tightly interwoven into our lives as ongoing shock, pain, loss and grief had to be worked through and lived with. A life of painful physical separation from Anna. However in time an unfolding understanding would show us that emotional and spiritual separation would never be necessary. For the tapestries of our lives had become inseparably interwoven. And now the threads of life's greater tapestry would continue to be worked until the day when the loom becomes silent and the shuttles cease to fly. Then, and only then, will we be able to appreciate the importance of *all* the colours worked in the weaver's skilful hands . . . the threads of black, red, blue, yellow, purple, green, gold . . . in the pattern *He* has planned. How our hearts yearn for that day!

---

[2]  Extract from 'The Prophet' by Kahlil Gibran Copyright © Random House, Inc. N.Y.

# 8

# A Frog with a Sore Throat

The road from the airport was festooned with flags. Draping every palm tree along the wide avenue, they flew to welcome the arrival of President Nelson Mandela to North Africa. North meets South! Government workers had toiled throughout the night to remove the colourful banners remaining from the last dignitary's visit – replacing them with the South African flag. Every second tree held high in its palms the national flag of this North African country. Such overt displays of nationalism would soon become a familiar part of my everyday life. Pictures of the country's president were everywhere – his portrait adorned the wall of nearly every shop and public establishment. He would even be stuck to each door of the maternity unit on which I would ultimately work. His face was the first to greet me on my arrival at immigration, following me through to baggage claims and the customs hall. He was obviously something big in this society . . . maybe even taking the place celebrities such as U2 and REM assumed in the hearts of Irish youth!

It was a swelteringly hot July afternoon with a Sahara gust blowing copious dusty sand into every crevice of my being. The coconut oil in my hair had long since melted, the hair itself increasing in weight as particles of sand joined the sticky mass. Perspiration streamed from every pore in my body – I was beginning to feel like Bob Marley's younger sister! This was at any rate a change from being asked by the customs man, who carried out a intrigued study of my hairstyle and violin case, if I was Nigel Kennedy's sister! 'If you heard me playing the violin you'd soon come to the conclusion that I'm not remotely related to such a famous musician.' I mused on how the reputation of people like Nigel Kennedy reaches even North Africa.

Closing my eyes I relaxed momentarily in the back seat of the car which had come to collect me at the airport. Imagining that these flags flapping in the wind and welcoming me to the fiery furnace of a North African summer were Irish ones. Disbelief surrounded the reality that I had finally arrived. After a long trail of cross-cultural and development studies leading to language learning in France, I was now one step nearer my final destination. Starting my work as a midwife in a southern location was still 'not yet' as these next months were to be invested in learning the local Arabic dialect. I tried not to focus too much on that mountain as my arrival had already been delayed owing to ill health. An explosive head on completion of my studies in France had required a brain scan 'in-transit' from a family holiday in Spain through Ireland to North Africa. Clearly my brain was full and pleading for a break while the problem of where to store all this new information was sorted out. A great way to be tackling yet another new language in such exhausting heat!

The journey from the airport took us up a small hill and along the outskirts of the capital's biggest park. The green vegetation was a refreshing sight in the midst of such dust and dryness. From that small incline a good view of this sprawling city could be enjoyed. A late afternoon haze sat over the endless expanse of dwellings which merged with the city centre, or *medina*, and continued on to the Mediterranean's edge. Here it joined the busy sea port which welcomed many cargo boats. Numerous minarets rising high into the deep orange sky reminded me of the strong Muslim culture I had come to work in. Sunday morning bells ringing out from an Irish country church were definitely something of the past. I was heading for a complete immersion into this new culture with its language and people very different from my own.

As we passed along the narrow road, my eyes followed a slope which gave way to a settlement of drab and basic dwellings. Down in a valley, once a remote rubbish dump for the capital's inhabitants, people had built homes from any suitable bricks, unwanted cement and scrap material they could find. No two dwellings were the same yet all sat on this once smouldering mass of refuse, a mound reclaimed on account of the population explosion in this sprawling city which grew bigger by the day – its foundations now sealed by years of sand and dust. Barefooted children playing on piles of compacted rubbish, laughed and danced against a background of washing strung on lines bridging the narrow gaps between dilapidated abodes. Women sat chatting on the roofs of unfinished homes characterized by steel rods projecting high into the sky from concrete walls. I found myself wondering what life was really like in the heart of this intriguing community. In the weeks that lay ahead there would be a precious opportunity to find out for myself.

Those early weeks of intense Arabic study were survived in a heat-induced daze. Temperatures of 40-45 degrees centigrade may be wonderful for sun-seeking tourists, but prove something of a nightmare for a language student like myself who dreams of an airconditioned room where the words just float into the brain while one sleeps! The subject of sleep seemed to occupy my every waking moment as I longed for the time when I could finally flop into bed under the cooling comfort of a fan.

Imagine you are a mosquito resting on the wall of my room – you too could experience a language lesson with Amjed. Wafting jasmine fragrance and a cooling breeze are some of the delights of having to study late into the evening. The final mosque call of the day, more study and bed lead into a night of feeding on my O-blood . . . after all remember you are a mosquito! Dawn's call to prayer rings out too soon after eyelids have finally been closed but prized cool hours of contemplation are a great incentive to rise early. Then for you the excitement of travelling to the office in my backpack as I fly through the park on my bike. Such a means of transport seems to cut down on the endless hassle previously experienced from the male population when walking alone. Close encounters with the MAD, MAD, MAD, drivers of this country demand nerves of steel. Aren't you lucky to be in my backpack so that watching the road is an optional extra? On arrival at the office you need to keep your eyes fixed on the board and look attentive – Amjed is a very sharp teacher. No possibility of micro sleeps around here, sorry! Only five minutes into the lesson and I'm dreaming of bed and chilled watermelon as temperatures in the classroom rise steadily. Not even the chugging electric fan's streams of cool air, pouring down the back of my neck, help maintain my concentration. There must be more to life than this! With renewed determination I focus on the final goal of being able to communicate in the local language. Whoops! In the meantime Amjed has noticed I'm flagging so makes me write on the board in Arabic script, Horror, Help! If you want to be spared such agony it's better to look alert at all times.

Amjed is a real perfectionist, taking all mistakes personally, basing this habit on the theory that he has failed to teach me properly. Assuring him that it's not his fault I'm Irish and mangle the Arabic language with my Dublin accent just proves fruitless. I can't exactly change 29 years of influence overnight. He could blame my mother – she should have got me a French and Arabic speaking 'au pair' when I was young. If I thought I sounded like a mouth-washing frog while painfully trying to deliver some intelligible French, I am fast sounding like a frog with a sore throat as Arabic introduces me to muscles I never even knew I had between my head and shoulders.

Coffee break remains the highlight of the morning during which a visit to the mail box reveals how many wonderful people have written. Wow! More letters. Coffee over and *splat*; Amjed has just noticed your presence and borrowed my *Guardian Weekly* to do the necessary. A bloody patch on the whitewashed wall and my messed-up newspaper will be a daily reminder of you. Aren't you so lucky to be put out of your misery? Some of us just have to plod on.

Karima's friendly nature extended a warm invitation to share in their family life for a month of my stay in the capital. Three months of intensive study were to be followed by immersion into the language and culture through living in a local North African home. I responded enthusiastically to the invitation with mounting excitement on hearing she lived in the heart of the fascinating valley settlement. This *was* going to be an experience!

Karima gave an outward impression of being rather 'happy-go-lucky' in her approach to life but her eyes gave away the lasting memories of painful years since she first left home as a teenager. A country lass brought up in the foothills of the Atlas mountains, she was promised to her first cousin in marriage. The glamour of such an unknown adventure swept her away to the heart of the capital where a house in this community was rented and pronounced 'home'. Excitement turned into sorrow as pregnancy and childbirth were struggled through far away from the support of her family. Hopes and dreams were smashed as the hardships of motherhood and poverty dug a deep pit of despair. The reproductive cycle continued with exhaustion, preventing Karima from living up to her husband's high expectations of a wife and mother. He became violent and started beating her and their small children.

During the eighth year of their marriage Karima's husband returned home one night in a trance and hit the youngest child's head on the stone floor. In a close-knit community nothing could be concealed. The neighbours alerted the police, the child was taken unconscious into hospital and the father locked up in prison. Karima was starting to see that evil spirits had possessed her husband. Borrowing money she sought the powers of a holy man to cast them out. On her husband's release from prison the beatings continued, with Karima slipping further and further into debt. Finally her husband was taken back into prison where a conclusion of mental illness was reached. The door was shut on him for life.

A lone mother in debt with four small children to care for, Karima was forced to find work. She proved to be excellent at cleaning other people's homes and so managed to feed and clothe her brood. As the children grew up and became teenagers, she found love and welcome security in her second husband Rachid. Yet he turned out to be something of a shrewd man who recognized Karima's potential in being accepted to clean the homes of foreigners. This meant money for the family and an easy life for him! Three more pregnancies marked the early days of this second marriage. Despite these young children's need of care, Karima was pushed out of the home to work. It was painful for her to leave the little ones to fend for themselves, yet fear of Rachid's anger left her no choice. Five days a week she shut the door early in the morning on Hazar, Hana, and Mohsen – ensuring all sharp implements were well hidden and a basic food supply left to sustain them until her return in the evening. And how they awaited that moment!

Knowing very little of Karima's background, and being limited in my communication skills, left me completely open to enjoy the delights of her friendship and the unique cultural experience of sharing in her family. Despite their many struggles in life, this family demonstrated a warm hospitality, and I felt so privileged to be part of it. Years of hardship had not given way to cankerous bitterness but left Karima thankful for each new day to be lived. She graciously accepted what she saw as the will of Allah and trusted that one day a reward of eternal rest awaited her. I marvelled at her strength of character.

The pathway to Karima's home took me along ever-narrowing streets paved with cobblestones. Men smoking through glass water pipes sat contemplating the world while others drank coffee and played cards. Children's laughter filled the streets as a huddle of devoted followers of the Muslim faith squeezed into a minute community mosque for prayer. The owner of the local necessities store soon got to know me – a strategically placed gas bottle outside his shop provided a crucial landmark in this maze of alleyways. It saved using a ball of string to find my way!

Late afternoons brought everybody home to this simple abode of two small main rooms, a tiny kitchen, toilet and open court-yard. Rachid and Karima, along with their three small children, made up fifty per cent of the household. Two of Karima's sons from her first marriage still lived with her along with two teenage girls estranged from their parents, and myself. We were ten in all along with the dog who very conveniently became my 5 a.m. alarm clock call.

Early evenings were invested in preparing a meal for all . . . my first introduction to North African cuisine! Seasonal vegetables were creatively served with bread from the local bakery. Squatting in the courtyard, next to the only source of water, we washed the dishes before retiring to while away the evening in front of the television. Two couches, a bulky china cabinet, and television filled the sitting room which would later be transformed into a bedroom for five. One by one the smaller children would drop off to sleep and be carried into the next room where a double bed accommodated Rachid, Karima, Hazar, Hana and Mohsen for the night. I was next to be overcome by exhaustion. My visitor status granted me the privilege of one of the couches to sleep on. Earplugs in place (in an attempt to block out the noise of the television and people talking), a pillow over my head (in a further attempt to block out noise and light), face turned to the wall, blanket pulled over my fully dressed body . . . and sleep. I can't say it was quality sleep but it was the best I could manage considering the circumstances. It was not unusual for the television to be watched until 2 a.m. . . . the audience not always appreciative of my snoring!

The fun began with the dawn mosque call as I endeavoured to find my way to the door in the pitch dark without stepping on somebody's head. If two bodies occupied the couches, I could count on at least three others lying on the floor between me and the door. All would have claimed their patch long after I had curled into a ball and given way to slumber. A few moments of listening to determine where breathing was coming from was my only guide through this obstacle course. I can't say I always got it right in my half-awake stupor but I certainly did my best. A grave mistake my first evening was to accept the use of Karima's bedroom to change into my pyjamas before settling down to sleep in the sitting-room. Karima appreciated that foreigners have night attire so did her best to make me feel at home. I only wish she had told me everybody else slept in their clothes! The following morning found me groping around helplessly in the dark to find my garments, identify them, and attempt to put them on in a presentable way before negotiating the obstacles and emerging through the door. Then there was the dog to humour if a safe passage was to be ensured to the outside world. With that final obstacle negotiated I was on my way to the office and language school . . . as the rest of the family snoozed on.

Green desert boots graced my feet during those weeks and emerged at the end of my month's stay richer in their cultural growth. This was thanks to the toilet which was just large enough to accommodate an adult bending over, with the floor space completely taken up by the ceramic body of a 'squatting' WC. Aim being very important when using such a latrine, good illumination is vital. Not only was Karima's toilet lacking in light but the latch on the door was also broken which meant a balancing act of aiming in the pitch dark while holding the door closed! My desert boots came out the worst for the experience thanks to my imprecise aim whilst balancing in a squatting position holding onto my trousers and the door. A shower from above was often preceded by added culture from below as I developed the habit of miscalculating the location of the foot platform. Whoops!

Weekends were for washing. Saturday was 'Omo' day when all the dirty clothes of the home's ten occupants were dragged out into the courtyard. From early morning until late afternoon Karima would squat over a huge tin basin, arms submerged in soapy water, and scrubbing hard. Wringing and endless rinsing followed before the spotless garments could be hung on the makeshift clothes line to dry. By the time there was no escaping a shower from dripping clothes while walking through the courtyard, Karima's hands were raw and bleeding from the effects of the bleach in the soap powder. Such were the added 'joys' of this backbreaking work.

Sundays were saved for the *hammam*. Travel guides paint a beautiful picture of the joys and delights of Turkish baths . . . yet describing my visit to the local wash house as 'joyful and delightful' would be something of an overstatement. Necessity was the driving force behind a weekly visit to the establishment owing to the complete lack of alternative washing facilities at home, an important opportunity to catch up on the local news and community gossip being an added incentive! So early on Sunday morning all the women would put together their buckets, soap, towels, tooth sticks, clean clothes, and the nominal entry fee necessary for the trip. The expedition could take up to four hours (advisable to leave your watch at home), the benefits usually lasted a week, yet the richness of the experience promised to endure a lifetime!

A large old building set in the heart of the community was where female young and old congregated on this morning. Built over a spring supplying copious clean water, it was *the* place to go for a good scrub. Charcoal fires belching smoke from tall chimneys were a reassuring sign of generous hot water on offer. The scent of oriental incense wafted out to greet us as we approached the tiled archway of these baths. A formal welcome accompanied the paying of our entry fee while a few curious glances were cast in my direction. Little did I know they came from the determined eyes of the chief scrubber delighting in the thoughts of making pulp of my tanned skin! Leaving behind the outside world with its familiar hustle and bustle of a Sunday morning market, a heavy olive-wood door opened up to a very different world: 'women only beyond this point'! I now found myself in a semi-lit room filled with women and children in varying degrees of undress: 'knickers only beyond this point!' Abundant buckets, bottoms, extra bulges and boobs passed through the next door enfolded in an atmosphere of chatter and laughter. Karima kindly showed me where to put my clothes and placed a pair of the statutory wooden clogs on my feet. Walking on wet marble floors gripping heavy blocks of seasoned sweaty wood attached to one's feet by means of a non-adjustable single leather strap ten times too big, is obviously an art acquired only through years of experience. Through the portal I skated – bucket, washcloth, soap, shampoo and henna grasped in one hand, the other holding onto Karima for dear life!

There stretched before me a white marble floor with a huge brick and tile vat of water taking up the main body of the room. A steady inflow of fresh, heated spring water bubbled up from the base of the vat. Spilling over onto the floor, it flowed in rivers down the passageways to numerous alcoves where scrubbing women congregated. Blue tiles ascended each wall to the skylight

on the ceiling – glittering in the brilliant sunshine pouring through this lone opening to the sky. As I paused to take in my surroundings, a continuous stream of semi-naked women and children came to fill their buckets. Returning to long olive-wood benches they rejoined the happy shampoo-and-green-soap party. Searching for a vacant bank on which to park ourselves, I marvelled at the way little children managed to stay upright on such a slippery floor, balancing such a heavy load of water, hanging onto knickers with failing elastic, amidst the push and shove of Sunday morning rush hour. I was feeling like a newborn lamb finding its wobbly feet!

Relief at being able finally to sit down was accompanied by unpacking of buckets and lots of organizational chatter. Hazar eagerly set off to collect some water while Karima mixed henna. It had seemed a very practical move to avail myself of these long hours in the *hammam* to put desired henna in my hair. The stress of life as a language student was starting to add to my collection of grey hairs! Karima's inexperience in henna application soon became evident – plopping a watery green cowpat-like mass on the top of my head for all to gawk at. Within a matter of minutes, aided by the very hot and humid atmosphere, it started to migrate down over my ears with rivers of orange-red fluid streaming down my neck dyeing my skin as it went. Panic welled up inside me as I remembered my commitment to lead part of that evening's church service. Eekkkk! I jumped to my feet in a mad panic to reach water before any serious damage was done. Skating across the marble floor I suddenly lost my balance as my right clog parted company with my foot – the leather strap twisting my ankle as it went. I was subsequently thrown into a skid landing in a heap beside the vat which had been my ultimate destination. An airborne bucket skipped in melodic fashion along the stone floor as lumps of flying 'cowpat' splashed very artistic designs on those beautiful blue tiles . . . .

I must have been in a state of 'elevated emotions and lowered intellect' following my ordeal when I agreed to a therapeutic massage by the hammam's resident masseuse. Yet what a relief to stretch out on a wooden plinth and enjoy welcome moments of relaxation! Some gentle background music and a fruit cocktail would have added the final touches as my thoughts drifted back to my backpacking days on those coconut islands in the gulf of Siam. My dream was rudely shattered when in place of gentle massaging hands doused in coconut oil, I found myself at the mercy of a rough steel wool-like mitt with seemingly the full weight of a battleship behind it! I hardly had time to look round at this 120 plus kilo dark-skinned 'mama' before she set to work, determined to make pulp of my delicate Irish skin. In no time at all she was rolling strings of what looked like wholemeal spaghetti between her mitt and my body. The pain of shearing off those upper layers of skin was endured in enforced silence as no breath could be snatched to protest beneath the full force of her body mass. I would not smell of perspiration for a week, she assured me!

Sitting with soggy wet knickers losing their elasticity by the minute, red blotchy skin looking like the setting sun, orange henna streaks down my ears and neck, mosaic bruises on my arms and legs, a thumping headache, sprained ankle, and piece of bark jammed between my teeth (a souvenir from a dental hygiene session), I was sorely tempted to pose the question: 'What on earth am I doing here?' In the end I concluded it was probably more constructive to marvel at the extent some people will go to in order to keep clean!

As a move further south in the direction of the Sahara loomed on the horizon, a painful goodbye to Karima and her family had to be said. Despite a deep longing to start my work as a midwife, to enjoy a good night's sleep and to enjoy some space to 'be', I was finding separation from this family painfully difficult. They had offered their best and provided me with a cultural insight I could have gained nowhere else. They had taught me how to stand in their culture, to listen, to smell and to see. I had been at the receiving end of so much yet felt paralysed by language and cultural barriers to offer anything in return.

On my last afternoon, walking through the narrow alleyways to Karima's house, I carried with me cake and Coke in an attempt to add a party tone to what was potentially going to be a sombre evening. A special meal of couscous with lamb had been prepared in my honour after which we followed the old routine of washing dishes and installing ourselves in front of the television. My treat was produced in the early evening to cheers of excitement from the children. As we partied a thunder storm of unusual strength and volume suddenly rolled overhead. Lightning flashed as the heavens poured forth torrential rain. We were happy to be huddled together inside – safe and dry from nature's elements.

As the evening progressed and we relaxed, a loud thud and crash startled us all. Rachid jumped to his feet and disappeared to investigate the source of the alarming noise. Returning only seconds later, he blurted out the distressing news that would change the whole tone of the evening. Under the weight of heavy rainfall, the roof of their bedroom had finally given way ... cement and scrap material now filled their only bed. Water poured through the ceiling. How thankful we were that no children had been asleep in the bed at the time of the accident! Tonight there would be no extra mattress for me to sleep on so I knew it was time to say farewell.

An unexpected break in the weather provided me with the opportunity to find my way back through the dark alleyways of this community to the 'outside' world where a hot chocolate, shower, fresh sheets and a good night's sleep were waiting for me. The abruptness of this prematurely forced farewell caught us all off guard. Still enfolded in the spirit of an unexpected party, the children played with the gateau box knocking the Coke bottle accidentally off the table. Rachid's attention continued to be absorbed by the ailing roof of their humble abode. So Karima and I were alone for a moment to share the pain of separation. My limited language allowed me to express only a basic 'thank-you' which fell pathetically short of my heartfelt expression of sincere gratitude. But something deep was communicated to me through Karima's holding embrace and flowing tears. As I ran through the streets, soft raindrops joined piercing tears rolling down my face.

For a long time to come I would feel like a frog with a sore throat as I grappled with the alien sounds of this Arabic language. My slipping and sliding on wooden *hammam* clogs was also guaranteed to continue metaphorically as I struggled to 'walk' with cultural insight and understanding. In the same way as a sore throat and sprained ankle hurt, so to 'plod on' and persevere is not the easiest road to tread. It was a road marked by the pain of frustration, misunderstandings, blunders, limitations, sweat and tears. Yet it would ultimately allow me to walk in deep sensitive understanding with folk like Karima. My sincere desire is to walk that rugged path of life with women like her, knowing we have so much to learn from each other. Together we can discover diamonds in the dust of our earthly existence – and how many diamonds there are to uncover!

# 9

# Love's Price Tag

Her name was Nabiha, but in the eyes of the other maternity unit staff she was merely 'the social case'. She would never be allowed to forget her position of disgrace during her hospital stay. As an unmarried mother, she was frowned upon, ridiculed, criticized and judged. No money to pay the nominal entry fee to the hospital meant scrutiny at administration level. No name to put down as father of the child meant police interrogation. No means to purchase a bottle of drinking water, clothes for the expected baby, or the necessary items for delivery, left her alone on the hospital bed clothed in a painfully thin cotton dress and lying beside a strikingly empty locker.

The pain of the unfamiliar uterine contractions seemed even more unbearable with the increasing sense of loneliness, lostness, and condemnation. 'Was the pain of rape not enough to cope with?' Not just the physical pain of the act itself, but also the emotional pain of lost virginity which would ensure a condemnation extending far beyond these days of hell in hospital to a condemnation for life.

Life, life, life, life ... a sharp kick inside her abdomen suddenly reminded her of the new life within her, the life which she had done her best to conceal these last nine months, and which was the product of that encounter which now condemned her for life. A new life that would in its turn be condemned, for it was after all the offspring of a 'social case' and would always be so marked by its obvious lack of right to a family name. An outcast before birth . . . .

The pain returned . . . insistent, unyielding, intensifying, merciless, fear-instilling, anger-provoking, despair-inducing, 'Help!' 'Help!' 'I need help,' a desperate plea to the outside world, and 'Help!' a silent cry from within – two lives closely interwoven yet divided by a wall of anger and hate; two lives pleading for help.

After many long hours help finally came in the only form offered – an external abdominal force pressing down strongly enough to speed up the passage of this new life through the birth canal into the waiting world – a cold, hostile and lonely world, where the warmth of its mother's body would no longer shield it.

Nabiha now found herself sharing the hospital bed with a naked daughter only a few hours old. Exhausted and spent by the ordeal of delivering this symbol of pain and bitterness into the world, she now had to share what had become her only shelter and place of refuge. At least she was still in possession of her light cotton dress (whatever its state) which prevented skin to skin contact with the intruder. At least she could turn her back, close her eyes and hope to awaken soon from this horrible nightmare.

But every time she opened her eyes the nightmare was still with her. How she longed for the energy to walk out of the hospital's front door and leave behind the reality of her present situation! Energy or no energy there were reams of papers to be filled in, many more questions to be answered, and important documents to be signed before a final escape could be made.

'But would those hospital doors really symbolize the end of this nightmare?' 'Could physical doors really close off the emotional pain of these last nine months?'

I first met Nabiha two days after the birth of her baby whilst I was endeavouring to do some health education with the newly-delivered mums. The cleaner informed me that we had another 'social case' on the ward. She would frequently go and stand over her exclaiming in a loud voice, 'God love her, isn't it a terrible shame what some girls' behaviour gets them into these days! God love her!'

Nabiha was forced to listen to many such remarks while awaiting the necessary discharge papers. She would then be free to return home, leaving her daughter to join the other five abandoned babies 'in waiting' for a place at the capital's orphanage. She lay asleep on her bed, back turned to her two-day-old daughter who seemed very unhappy about something. In fact first impressions were of a mutually unhappy pair. A little probing revealed that this had been a crying baby since delivery, and peace came only when she fell into an exhausted sleep. The other mums in the ward seemed relieved that after their 24-hour compulsory stay in hospital they would be free to return to the relative tranquillity of their own homes.

I was upset to discover the primary source of the baby's discontent – hunger! To add to the misery of not having been fed since delivery, she was naked and soiled, having received no care or attention whatsoever. In an effort to control and use constructively my feelings of upset, I started gently to explain to Nabiha her daughter's basic needs.

'You see Nabiha, a newborn baby is reliant on someone to meet its need of food, warmth, cleanliness, stimulation, and love. If these needs aren't met it will surely die. At this moment your baby is totally dependent on *you*!' The response was fast and forceful:

'Food! But I have no milk yet, so how can I possibly breast-feed her?' I gently explained that sucking is necessary to stimulate milk production and that what was now in her milk ducts was adequate for the baby's needs during its early days of life. 'There's a lot more in there than you think!' I remarked in an effort to lighten the increasingly tense atmosphere. As I supported the baby's head, allowing its mouth to come into contact with Nabiha's right nipple, the sucking reflex took over as all her energy was put into gulping down the drops that would help sustain her life. After a few minutes of frantic non-stop sucking, the babe settled into a more civilized pattern of suck, pause, suck, pause, suck, pause . . . . Nabiha's explosion continued:

'Warmth! But I have no clothes to put on her, so she will just have to stay naked.' One of the other mums in the ward, over-hearing our conversation, quickly offered Nabiha a simple cotton vest which allowed the baby to pass from the classification 'naked' to 'clothed' . . . even if the garment offered was far from adequate.

'Cleanliness! How can I possibly keep her clean when I have no soap or water?' An empty plastic bottle (refillable in the bathroom at the end of the ward) accompanied by a small cube of basic green soap, soon offered a solution to that problem.

'Stimulation and love! How can you expect me to love the product of brutality?' Nabiha's chilling remark caught me off guard and took me totally by surprise. She had given the impression of being such a quiet person, silently shouldering the bombardment of ridicule and condemnation since her admission. Now I was being given a little glimpse of what was really going on inside. The soft hum of suck, pause, suck, pause, started to penetrate the ensuing marked silence and drew my attention back to the life still cradled in my arms.

My heart genuinely went out to Nabiha in all she had gone through and had yet to go through. Outlining 'stimulation and love' as two basic needs of the newborn was something I did very much out of habit. As a midwife, my management of the newborn has always included emphasis on the need for a mother to talk to her baby, touch, stimulate and love it. In the same way that milk is essential for sustaining and promoting physical growth, so stimulation and love are essential for sustaining and promoting emotional and spiritual growth. Both basic, and both essential.

I now found myself faced with two victims of circumstance, both with deep needs screaming to be met. Nabiha's anger and bitterness was slowly becoming my own: anger in response to what rape had done to her as a woman. Her lost virginity now meant she could be married off only as 'substandard', if at all. In a culture governed by a religion that clearly says: 'An unmarried woman is only half a woman', Nabiha would no doubt accept any condition linked to an offer of marriage. Only then would she be able to experience some relief from her shame. But my anger was also a response to her psychological trauma being worked out in rejection and neglect of her newborn baby. My anger was interwoven with a desire to minister healing love to both mother and child – my heart was torn.

Whatever her background or story, the inflexible local system required Nabiha to breast-feed and care for her baby for as long as she was in hospital. On her discharge, care of the baby would be handed over to the ward staff (usually the cleaners) who made sure a full bottle of infant formula was continuously propped up in the baby's mouth. No one wasted time pondering the emotional needs of the mother and the subsequent trauma of separation once the bonding process with her child had begun. The hospital doors stood as symbols of a threshold over which she would pass in her return to life as 'normal', when 'out of sight' became a comfortable 'out of mind'.

It seemed emotionally cruel to expect Nabiha to breast-feed and care for her baby when separation was inevitable. The option of letting the ward staff fulfil the caring role was taken when her persistent refusal to feed the child resulted in jaundice and dehydration setting in on day four. I personally felt it was ultimately the kindest option for both mum and baby.

However on day seven following delivery something changed in Nabiha's attitude. She went looking for her daughter (who was with the other abandoned babies), quietly returned to her hospital bed cradling her and started breast-feeding. She then washed her little vest, laying it out in the sun to dry, and cleaned her skin with gentle strokes accompanied by soft affectionate murmuring. Observing from a distance, I watched for a few days trying to determine exactly what was happening. A spontaneous explanation was soon offered as Nabiha quietly told me that her daughter needed the best possible start to life, especially as she would soon have to fight her way through that life alone. The stronger she became during these early days the better her chance of ultimate survival.

In this commitment to care for her daughter, Nabiha was offering her all as a mother – her all in a society which in turn offered her only one option: to walk away and leave her child behind when discharge from hospital was finally approved. The depth of their increasing bonding showed as Nabiha chose a name for her daughter 'Yasmin' – meaning beautiful scented flower. Nabiha's devotion now extended even further to the offer of care

until a place in the capital's orphanage could be found. But little did she or I know that would not be for four and a half months! Months during which Nabiha became part of our working life on the maternity unit with people growing in respect for her as they watched the painfully difficult task to which she had committed herself. Yasmin breast-fed beautifully, putting on plenty of weight and soon responding with a smile to the fountain of love and stimulation she received from her mother. In place of the worn cotton vest Nabiha stitched together a simple dress from scraps of old torn bed sheets. We saw the outworking of a love which grew by the day.

Secretly we all started to dread the day when 'they' would come from the capital and take Yasmin away. Word finally came through that a place had become vacant and a car would soon be sent to collect the babe.

During those dreaded days of waiting Nabiha shared with me that she would love to be able to keep Yasmin but her family would have her back only without the baby. I clearly understood there was the question of the family's honour to take into consideration, an honour that would undoubtedly be shattered by the presence of an illegitimate child. But there was also the question of poverty. Nabiha's family were rural farmers living off the land. Four stone walls and a dilapidated roof comprised their home, with no electricity and the nearest water pump five kilometres away. An extra mouth to feed would put too great a burden on the already meagre food supplies. Such poverty meant that Nabiha had no money to 'go it alone'. She had no choice.

Knowing the situation in the orphanage where Yasmin would most probably be going didn't allow me to reassure Nabiha that her baby would be well looked after and loved. The only encouragement I could offer her was that she had ensured Yasmin got the best start to life. Thanks to a mother's loving care she was now a strong and healthy four and a half month old in the best position possible to face alone the hostile world awaiting her. Nabiha had unquestionably offered and given her best.

It was a Thursday morning when a man came to collect a 'female infant of four and a half months old'. No need to know the baby's name: so long as the mother's name was the same as that written on the collection papers and the baby girl was of that age, his job was done. Everybody took a deep breath as the assistant leaned forward to take Yasmin. She started to cry sensing the distress of her mother and the hostility of the male stranger. Nabiha's anguish was heart-wrenching to witness as the world stepped in and thrust a wedge between a preciously-bonded mother and daughter. Their bond had grown through the experience of pain – the pain of rape, of ridicule, of rejection, of labour, of childbirth, of maternal commitment. And it was now being torn apart by yet another experience of pain – the pain of separation.

*And ever has it been that love knows not its own depth until the hour
of separation.*

Kahlil Gibran.[1]

This was the hour of separation and the pain was unbearable, so
crippling that no words of comfort could be found for that which
only tears seemed capable of expressing. My humanity screamed
from within me to do something. I knew this separation was for
life as it would never be possible to trace Yasmin again. She would
soon become just another number in a vast system. I knew she
wouldn't be cared for as her mother had cared for her over the
last few months. I knew there would be times when illness would
threaten her life. I knew she would be starved of love and
stimulation . . . but deep in my heart I knew too that Nabiha had
no choice but to let her go.

A further shattering came on a personal level as I was con-
fronted by my powerlessness to do anything. Even as an affluent
Westerner with all my skills as a nurse and midwife, my years of
overseas experience, my deepening appreciation of other cultures,
my understanding of Islam as a religion, I was still powerless to
offer an alternative. My Western 'power' fell outside the boundaries of this culture. My status here was merely that of 'guest',
allowed right of entry into this culture's code of practice only in
response to an extended invitation. The distinct lack of invitation
at that moment was marked.

My humanity now screamed beyond 'do something' to '*say*
something'. As if my physical incapacity to respond wasn't
distressing enough, I was now hit by my inability to respond at
a much deeper level where there are no cultural boundaries. For
God's love in me is a free agent unbound by cultural invitation.
The 'royal' invitation was there to pour healing love into this
heart-rending situation before me, but I found no words to cut
through my emotional numbness and devastating feelings of
helplessness. I wanted to say 'God loves you Nabiha' but it

---

[1]  Extract from 'The Prophet' by Kahlil Gibran, Copyright © Random
House, Inc. N.Y.

seemed miserably inadequate in its simplicity. Experience of God's love was all right for me. But if like Nabiha your experience is of a religion of submission and acceptance, with life's painful trauma deemed the will of almighty Allah, then to be told 'God loves you' at the point of intense struggle is meaningless. All I could do was stand there and allow my tears to flow in silence.

In silence I wept as I watched Yasmin being carried across the threshold to a new life of living separation. In silence I wept as I watched Nabiha eventually find strength to pick up the discarded little dress that would remain the only physical reminder of a deep love grown out of such pain. In silence I wept as I watched Nabiha too cross the threshold in a return to 'normal' life. In silence I continued weeping as I realized how my tears had carried me across a threshold into the hearts and lives of a very precious North African mother and baby.

# Ten

# Three for the Price of One

The walk to work took me across open fields awaiting winter and spring when they could prove their fertility in nurturing precious crops of wheat. My attention was drawn to the deep cracks in soil resembling fired clay worked by a potter, cracks that were now a refuge for tiny lizards scuttering from my path. This journey provided me with an opportunity to focus my thoughts on the day that lay ahead. My ears soon 'tuned in' to the cries of women in labour ringing out across the fields from open hospital windows. I never knew what was going to confront me when I walked through the doors of the regional maternity unit. Habiba's face was the first to greet me that sweltering hot July morning. It was only 6.50a.m. but already the temperature was 32 degrees centigrade. With a busy and sweaty day guaranteed, I made a conscious effort to guard the memories of cooler hours enjoyed since dawn when I first rolled out from underneath my mosquito net.

'Please do something as I'm in so much pain' – Habiba's beseeching face snapped me back into the reality of the moment. I was immediately struck by her extra large abdomen. 'My goodness you have a big tummy! Are you sure you're not expecting more than one baby?' slipped off the end of my tongue in Arabic without thinking. The switch to Arabic marked the start of a day's work conducted in this brain-draining language. Another switch, this time to French, would be necessary later for report-writing. The distress of the painful contractions accompanied by the horror of my suggestion threw Habiba into a panic.

The size of her abdomen nearly threw me into a panic as I realized she was now my sole responsibility. I'd seen the midwife from the night shift slip out of the front door within seconds of my arrival with, 'There's no obstetrician available until 8.30 a.m.' as her parting shot. Great! Had time permitted, I might have toyed with the idea of retracing my steps across the fields to the security of home. Habiba's pleading face left no room for that.

Within five minutes of my arrival at work Habiba was on the delivery table for assessment. Childbirth was imminent and the size of the presenting head reassured me that this was not an outsize baby with potential for getting its shoulders stuck on the way out – very important when the option of surgical intervention would not be available for at least another two hours. What it *did* mean though was a 99% chance that more than one baby was to be expected. I hurriedly added a few extra cord-clamps to my basic delivery box containing two artery forceps, scissors and a needle-holder. As I fumbled around for something to wrap the babies in, Habiba started pushing, the pouch of amniotic fluid surrounding the baby burst and Sufean was delivered into my waiting hands. It was 6.58 a.m. He soon filled his lungs with life-giving air and yelled, ruling out the need for the emergency assistance of a paediatrician (no doubt unavailable anyway at that hour of the morning). Once he was weighed, labelled 'Twin A', dried, wrapped up warm, and placed on his side facing in our direction, I returned to assess what was coming next.

Another little head was awaiting the return of expulsive uterine contractions in order to complete its journey into the world. A second pouch of amniotic fluid burst, one big push from Habiba, and Salah 'Twin B' was delivered into my welcoming hands. It was 7.08 a.m. He was determined not to be outdone by his brother so yelled twice as loudly. With an inner sigh of relief I once again went through the procedure of weighing, labelling, drying, wrapping, and placing him on his side next to his brother and facing us. Habiba's abdomen still seemed a bit too large for comfort so I returned to see what was coming now!

'Triplet C' was patiently awaiting its turn to journey out of the warm and safe environment of Habiba's womb. And wait he did as uterine contractions momentarily went on strike and every minute seemed like an eternity. A quick glance over my shoulder reassured me of Sufean's and Salah's nice pink facial skin. They seemed snug and content in their early moments of earthly life. The unexpected lull in the proceedings gave me a moment to get in touch with what I had stumbled into. It was just twenty minutes since my arrival at work and I was already delivering a third triplet! Triplet deliveries were something I had only read about in obstetrics textbooks. Now I had to pinch myself into believing I was actually in the process of conducting one. The simplicity was striking but recalling the many risk factors clearly outlined in those textbooks, guaranteed me a few more grey hairs. Here were Habiba and I with a basic instrument box and shredded pieces of an old cotton dress serving as drapes to receive the babies. An uncontrollable nervous giggle came from within me. If this had been happening in England where I trained as a midwife Habiba and her three babies would be the centre of an incredible fuss. The consultant obstetrician might well have conducted this delivery himself with his registrar in attendance. There would be endless supplies of sterile drapes, gowns, gloves, cotton wool, and warm antiseptic solution. Habiba would have epidural anaesthesia, be connected to at least two intravenous infusions, her babies assessed by means of monitors recording each individual heartbeat along with the strength and frequency of her uterine contractions. There would be three paediatricians to welcome the babies, three midwives offering assistance, three neonatal resuscitation tables to place them on, and three incubators in which to place them finally. There would be a ward assistant as 'runner' for anything the team might need. The labour-ward sister would be ensuring all ran smoothly and coordinating the availability of operating-theatre facilities in the event of an emergency. In fact Habiba would have been a case for elective Caesarean section as the risks of a normal delivery would have been considered too high. Simplicity was beautiful for as long as we stayed clear of complications, at which point simplicity would become our worst nightmare. An infection-infested fly landing on my sweaty brow brought me back to the reality of the more unwelcome aspects of this simple environment.

The 'popping' of another amniotic sack accompanied the return of expulsive contractions. Two pushes and Sabir was safe in my hands. Habiba's abdomen shrank to an acceptable size and I felt assured the placenta was all that remained. Habiba, in a state of stunned silence gazed at her newborn sons.

There had been no time to prepare her psychologically for this event. Communication between us had been minimal as all my effort had been concentrated on the mechanics of safely delivering these precious lives. At least she had delivered the right sex to be highly respected in this Arab culture. I could detect a ray of contentment breaking through the dark cloud of shock. 'This is what they call three for the price of one,' remarked the cleaner who had come to see what needed mopping up. My attention now turned to assessment of the other eight women in labour left under my care. It was 7.20 a.m. – 30 minutes into my working day.

The paediatric ward became Habiba's home for the next five weeks as she cared for her premature sons each of whom weighed one and a half kilos (just over three pounds). The ward was also the place where our friendship grew as we passed long hours together pondering over and implementing the best care for her babies. My commitment to teaching this rural woman how to meet the deep needs of her three sons during these vulnerable early weeks of life, came as a natural extension of my commitment to see them safely delivered into this world. Without that commitment I knew their lives would not be sustainable. Yet such a commitment took me out of my defined field of responsibility into the sensitive environment of an existing local paediatric team. My journey to and from work on the maternity unit now took me via the paediatric ward.

Habiba was a very plain girl brought up in a rural region 60 kilometres from the town where the regional maternity unit was based. Illiterate and married young to her first cousin she was already mother to an eighteen-month-old son. She and her husband worked the land and they as a family lived off it. Their home was a basic four wall brick building with a flat roof. They had no electricity and a walk of 2 kilometres to the nearest well. Four goats, the family's prize possession, provided their daily quota of milk. During Habiba's pregnancy her husband had spent all their savings on a sheep to be slaughtered at delivery of a male infant. A party was planned for Sufean's, Salah's, and Sabir's homecoming.

The anticipated problems of the premature plagued these three new babes during their first week of life. Weight loss was expected but when it passed the acceptable percentage of their birth weight, diplomatically thought-out questions were posed. The paediatrician had decided that breast-feeding 'on demand' was to be their source of nutrition. Their initial performance at breast-feeding was impressive but after a few feeds it became apparent that the strength to sustain the sucking action required for adequate breast-feeding was lacking. They tired easily, lost interest in feeding, slept for long hours and their body temperature dropped. The weight loss continued.

Two-hourly feeds requiring minimal effort were necessary for these premature babies to put all their energy into weight-gain. On day seven the paediatrician agreed that nasogastric tubes should be inserted to allow the monitoring of their milk intake. Habiba was taught how to check that the tubes were still safely placed in the stomach, hand-express her precious breast milk into a beaker, measure out the required amount and pass the milk down the tubes by way of a syringe. She continued two-hourly feeds throughout the day and night without fail, recording each one by means of a cross on a chart. I was deeply impressed by this 'simple' girl's capacity to engage so excellently in such new and alien procedures. It was a delight to teach this uneducated mother the importance of hand washing, cleaning of utensils and sterilizing them in a very makeshift sterilizing unit. Her motherly instinct was so strong and her dedication to her babies so deep that it rendered her a 'sponge' for all she needed to learn to give of her best. The maternal bond grew as Habiba's giving was rewarded by a response, or two, or three!

The second menace that plagued these three during their early days of life was their inability to maintain their body temperature. Low nutritional intake during the first week of life had not allowed any extra calories for warmth. Their skin was blue, cold and clammy to touch which was a cause for great concern. Hypothermia accompanied excessive weight loss and presented as lethargy with excessive hours spent sleeping. It seemed incredible that in daytime temperatures of 40–47 degrees centigrade anyone could be so cold! These babies needed an environment providing consistent heat 24 hours a day. A welcome drop of 20 degrees centigrade at night may be life-preserving for us adults during unbearably hot summer months but it was life-threatening for these scraps. Missing parts were found for an out of use incubator which was miraculously brought back into action. With great rejoicing Sufean, Salah and Sabir were placed side by side in the incubator. They seemed subconsciously to relax back into the familiar environment of their mother's womb where they were warm, well-fed and in close contact with each other.

With an increase in body temperature and calories came a marked increase in incubator activity levels. The usual pattern of events went something like this: following a feed Salah would start getting bored so decide to give Sufean a kick or two. Sufean, not very appreciative of being disturbed would pull Salah's nasogastric tube out of place. Sabir would get excited by all the activity and invariably pee all over the inside of the incubator. Evacuation of all three followed to facilitate clearing up the mess, after which Habiba would give them all a rundown on the rules of community living. It was fascinating to watch their behaviour improve momentarily as her tone of voice communicated the depth of her displeasure. She was proud of her sons and adamant they would not behave like this in public! The pattern of activity in the incubator was familiar to Habiba. She could now identify what had gone on over the last few months '*in utero*' between the three brothers. Salah apparently had a track record of kicking. He always chose the early hours of the morning when all was calm and quiet to do something about his boredom. Sufean would respond by pulling on Salah's umbilical cord and Sabir's excitement caused him to take a big gulp of amniotic fluid setting off a bout of hiccups. Habiba had the individual characters of her boys well 'sussed out'. Salah was the fighter of the three, Sufean the bullied and Sabir the pacifist.

As the days passed in devoted loving care, the weighing scales became a source of great encouragement. Every half ounce counted as these babies climbed their way back to their birth-weight and beyond. Powdered infant formula was introduced as Habiba's supply of breast milk was not proving adequate for the needs of all three. It was hoped that such an augmentation of milk would be short-lived as we knew the huge risks that went with bottle-feeding in a rural setting.

It wasn't easy for Habiba to be in hospital for such an extended period of time – 60 kilometres was a long way for her husband to come to visit from a rural station. Every day seemed like an eternity to him without his wife and children, Ali (their other son) having moved in with his grandmother until Habiba's discharge. Within two weeks of her confinement the pressure was on for Habiba to return home. Gentle explanation of the risks to the babies eased the situation somewhat but we all doubted whether the father would agree to let them stay until they had reached the minimum discharge weight of 2 kilos (4lbs 4 ozs). For him Habiba's stay in hospital meant the loss of someone to cook, clean, wash clothes, look after Ali, tend to the goats, and pick the precious ripe almonds. No man could take a woman's place in the home. Habiba was sorely missed. Yet every extra day in hospital was crucial for these babies if they were going to survive in the hostile world awaiting them.

It was a Friday morning marking the end of five weeks of friendship-building with Habiba. On arriving at work I found her all packed and ready for discharge. My heart sank. Her husband couldn't bear the separation any longer and threatened to divorce her if she didn't come home. Salah had reached his target weight for discharge with the other two falling short by 120 grammes (4 ounces). To supplement breast-feeding, bottles of infant formula were still needed augmenting the many dangers already awaiting these precious lives. I understood that Habiba had little choice if she wanted to have a home and husband to return to. I rested in the reassurance that she now had a good grasp of the care and standard of hygiene necessary if her babies were to continue to thrive. She was the key figure in determining their future. My responsibility was coming to a end.

But before discharge there was one area of responsibility needing addressing: 'Now Habiba I need to talk to you about something very important – family planning. You see, as from next week you run the risk of becoming pregnant again.' She didn't seem too keen to adopt any method on offer reassuring me she would use the calendar method to stay clear of 'at risk' times of the month. I knew such a method was doomed to fail before the return of regular menstrual periods. My case continued: 'You now have you hands full with four beautiful children to look after and it would be a disaster if you fell pregnant again too quickly. Especially considering you may have five babies next time!' Her look of horror signalled that the message had struck home. We were down in the family planning clinic within half an hour.

Habiba and the new additions to her family arrived home amid great celebration. A party was thrown for the extended family and all the community. The sheep was slaughtered in Sufean's, Salah's and Sabir's honour and its blood painted on the door posts for protection from evil spirits. Amulets (charms) were attached to their clothes to ward off the effects of the 'evil eye'. People were coming and going offering Habiba their congratulations yet noticeably avoiding any overt admiration of her new babies. To do so would be tempting fate.

The music got louder as the dancing got faster and the dark blanket of night wrapped itself around the party. Habiba's attention turned to breast-feeding Salah, entrusting the care of dozing Sufean and Sabir into her mother-in-law's hands. Such a woman was a highly respected member of the community and her wealth of experience in traditional practices was regarded as invaluable. Modern trends were new and inferior in her opinion yet pride would not give way to admitting her ignorance of these 'fads'. As Salah contentedly nursed at Habiba's breast this 'wise' woman decided to prove her worth by preparing a feeding bottle for Sufean and Sabir. She took well water from the porous storage jar, poured it into the feeding bottle, added an indeterminate number of scoops of powdered milk, and threw in a few spoons of sugar for good measure. After all, these little scraps needed fattening up! As the solution went through the rubber teat and into the gastro-intestinal tract of the two famished boys, Habiba nursed on in blissful ignorance.

It was early next morning that Habiba first became aware of a change in the state of Sufean's and Sabir's health. Both had vomited since their 6.00 a.m. feed and they now had a bout of unpleasant diarrhoea. The diarrhoea and vomiting persisted throughout the day and became accompanied by lethargy, disinterest in feeding, and sleeping long hours. Habiba's motherly instinct told her that something was seriously wrong yet she could recall no particular reason for such a dramatic change in their state of well-being. She had faithfully followed all the rules of hygiene in preparation of feeds and feeding utensils. She had even bought bottled water, boiling it on a charcoal fire before using it for feeds. Her thoughts steered away from such a source of infection to the spiritual realm – 'Could somebody possibly have cast the 'evil eye' on her two babies when she wasn't looking?' To be the mother of three such lovely boys was bound to be the source of much envy in the female community. 'Or could it have been the photographs that midwife took on their discharge from hospital?' Cameras were well known to have the power of stealing blessing from the spirit of the person or even inflicting a curse.

Dawn broke, marking 36 hours since the celebrated homecoming. Habiba made her way to a *marabout* (holy man) shrine in order to seek spiritual advice and assistance concerning the condition of her now critically ill sons. She was given new amulets to place on the babies' clothes and assured they were rich in blessing and healing power. The activity of evil spiritual forces jealous of her beautiful sons was confirmed. The *jinn* are such envious spirits, she was reminded.

That evening as Salah fed vigorously from Habiba's breast Sufean and Sabir lay dying on a wool rug draping the concrete floor. Their tiny bodies had once again become cold and blue, their eyes sunken and their skin flaccid. As though united from womb to grave they gasped their last breath in unison, rendering their bodies pale and lifeless. The 'bullied' and the 'pacifist' had given up the game.

*Maktub* – written since the beginning of time. Habiba pondered on this painful acceptance of Allah's will. The cost had been high. Maybe Allah the all merciful would grant her the ongoing presence of her third son now nursing at her breast. Maybe his mercy would appreciate how her joy at
            'THREE FOR THE PRICE OF ONE'
had now become her painful
            'ONE FOR THE PRICE OF THREE'.

# 11

# Soaring on Eagles' Wings

With the shifting shadows of dawn the eagle took flight, leaving the nooks and crannies of the cliff face, spreading her wings and setting her curved beak to the heights. There the first rays of the morning sun caught her cream and brown feathering, turning it into a cloak of glistening gold which she wore with majestic pride, confident of her position above all other birds. As she continued upwards the full expanse of her vast wings was realized. With two graceful beats the power of those feathered sails carried her high to meet the morning winds. She rode the winds as long as they carried her towards her destination; then, parting company with them, she willed her wings into motion once more, proclaiming to the wakening world with a shriek of exhilaration the depth of her experience. She was soaring in the heights – a privilege reserved for the few.

On that cool morning my mum and I shared in the eagle's shriek of exhilaration as our hearts and minds identified with her soaring. Quality time together had been lacking in recent years. My heart for the mothers and babies in countries 'on the way to development' had taken me to African shores, while Mum's heart for the broken and hurting lives of children in the Emerald Isle demanded her all at home. The oceans that lay between us meant living an often painful physical separation stretching across months and years. Yet nothing could drive a wedge into our deep and ever-growing intimate bond of love and friendship. Shared moments of solitude in a God-given friendship such as ours were treasured – especially when they were soaked in the beauty of creation. So we relished every minute of an unexpected spring holiday during which my life and work in North Africa could be shared. There were even days to explore the beauty of this country's unspoilt corners – such as that where we now found ourselves.

We had risen at dawn to descend into the valley tucked away in the cliffs of the Atlas mountains running across North Africa. An oasis flourishing with dark green date palms gave way to the sandstone remains of a deserted town. Through the valley ran a dry river-bed last overburdened with torrential floods in the late 1960's. Devastating rains from high in the mountains had taken this peaceful town by surprise one winter's night. The waters washed many still sleeping from their homes – never to return. What remained of the now deserted town stood as a memorial to the lives claimed in that freak torrent. Their spirits joined those of the dead holy men whose final resting places were the only buildings reconstructed amid the desolation. White-painted domes marked these *marabout* shrines to which people yet flocked. Petitioning for the souls of departed loved ones still continued, consistent and sincere.

As we walked together along the narrow alleyways in the morning coolness of the mountain air, the walls of deserted homes demanded our respectful silence, and as we emerged from the old town the vast dry river bed summoned us to sit, basking in the caressing rays of the rising sun and drinking in the beauty of the luscious oasis 'en face'. As we scanned the panorama nomadic Bedouin tents scattered along the paths leading up out of the valley came into focus. As yet no sign of life was evident beneath the burgundy and chocolate brown stripes of their waxed camel-hair homes. So as we sat, it was from the ridges of the awesome cliffs around us that the first signs of this morning's life came. The grand eagle's magnificent flight captured our gaze and thoughts.

While sitting captivated by the eagle an overwhelming urge gripped me. Simple yet profound words formed in my mind – their familiarity to me making the need to verbalize them seem pointless and somewhat confusing. 'Surely Mum had known, if not heard them, many times before?' Yet out the compelling words poured! 'You know Mum, when I look at you I see everything in the world I could hope to be.' Her response finally broke the stunned silence: 'Well Lizzy, that is the most beautiful thing anybody has ever said to me!' It was now my turn to be stunned into silence as I suddenly realized that Mum had no idea of the beautiful person she was and how that beauty had touched the lives of so many people. Over the years her life had been completely given over to the filling of God's Spirit – nothing of 'self' remained. Her selfless giving was being used to minister healing to the lives of many hurting people. Watching from the outside we could all see it so clearly – a fact which made it incredible that she lived totally oblivious of it. When I studied her Christ-like character I truly did see everything I could hope to be . . . yet felt such a long way from attaining. Her example encouraged me to keep my eyes focused on the 'heights'.

'You know, Lizzy, I see so many of my dreams fulfilled in you.' I was totally unprepared for the heartfelt words. Silence once again. I had never viewed my work as a midwife with 'the poor, powerless and pregnant' of this world, as a fulfilment of another's dreams. For the first time I glimpsed how a godly 'investment' handed down from generation to generation matures in the life of another. I pondered the importance of expressing our appreciation of those whom we love. How easy it is to assume people know how we feel about them.

As we climbed back out of the valley the eagle once again captured our attention, drawing us to a halt. This time it was to witness pre-breakfast flying lessons for the nest's young inhabitant. His day had come! High up on the cliff face the mother bird nosed her unsuspecting little one out of the nest. The frightened bundle, after a feeble effort to suspend himself in mid air, fell into a nose dive, gaining more momentum the longer he failed to stretch out his tiny wings. Halfway through his descent he started to get some idea of what his feathered accessories might be for and made a weak effort to use them, but the attempt proved powerless to break such a rapid fall, and the descent continued. As the rocky ground below came closer and closer, the terrified little creature struggled in a final attempt to get his wings working – to no avail. Pitiful cries of abandonment now echoed through the valley as his fate seemed sealed. The reality of a shattering encounter with the unmercifully sharp stony boulders below was just seconds away.

Yet all the time the mother eagle hovered overhead – out of sight but watching attentively. At the last moment she swooped underneath the baby bird breaking his fall – Phew! That was close! Happy landing on a feather cushion!

And now the ascent could begin . . . those vast strong wings starting a gradual climb back to the heights. All the time the baby bird occupied his cushioned position as recuperating passenger. Higher and higher the great eagle climbed as the fledgling relaxed and gained new courage. Within the security of his mother's feathers he started to try his own feathered attachments. Yes, he could stretch them out! And with that stretching they caught the wind: firstly the powerful waves of back-draught from his mother's wing movement – and then the full winds of nature itself, lifting him light and airborne yet still secure in the assurance of his mother's great frame directly underneath. Reassured, he gave way to a growing desire to move his wings. Gaining strength and confidence he began to rise high up off his mother's back. With an ectatic sense of freedom he suddenly realized he was flying! He now soared with his mother exulting in his new independence; she followed shrewdly in his shadow encouraging him yet recognising his vulnerability and weakness. Her feather cushion would always be there for him.

Our eyes riveted in amazement, we absorbed every part of this spectacle. As our climb continued Mum stopped for a moment to put into words the way the scene had touched her. 'You see, Lizzy, the view from the heights is exhilarating and awesome but it can only truly be appreciated after an experience of growth which takes place down there in the valley.' How a little eagle lived that reality on his day of flying lessons!

The memories of that precious morning tucked away in the Atlas mountains remained vivid as yet another North African summer was survived and autumn found me on leave in Ireland. I went home to a house where it seemed as if elastic walls and elastic meals accommodated the many people who passed in and out through our front door.

The kitchen was the hub of our home's life and activity. My enduring picture of Mum is of her standing at the kitchen sink kneading bread whilst conducting an impromptu counselling session by means of a portable phone tucked under her chin. A small child would be sitting at her feet sucking its thumb and gently stroking the smoothness of her tights – all to the background hum of 'The Archers' on BBC Radio 4, the pressure cooker whistling away on the hob, and the intermittent ringing of the front door bell heralding the arrival of yet another caller.

A small tray would be laid on the table for great Aunt Nora's mid-morning tea – at ninety years of age she was the latest addition to, and most senior member of our family. The extremes of vulnerable youth and old age were well represented in our home. And both loved our ever-increasing cat population!

As the days closed in the sumach tree on our front lawn shed a blanket of fiery red and golden leaves. My introduction of North African spices into the family cuisine provided us all with 'built in' central heating as cold weather hit with a vengeance. Yet in those damp, dark, dreary days, one could always find warmth and security in the heart of Mum's kitchen. It radiated a loving welcome to all – providing a comforting shelter to many who sought refuge from the strong, cutting forces of life's approaching winter. On coming home I often curled up in the big chair beside the solid fuel cooker just to enjoy 'being' in this nurturing environment. It was saturated in love and in a godly healing presence which my whole body soaked up like a sponge. My thoughts drifted back to that baby eagle in the security of his nest . . . beautifully protected from the cliff face, the sharp boulders, the strong forces of nature. How idyllic it would be to sit here forever! Fat chance! I had a sneaking feeling my armchair was only to be enjoyed for a time . . . I was soon to be nudged out.

That 'push' came only a few days later when I had taken over at the kitchen sink: vegetable soup on the hob, children playing at my feet, cats on the windowsill, great-Aunt Nora drinking her late morning cuppa, postman delivering letters, milkman requesting payment of his bill, when the phone rang. Holding the fort until Mum's and Dad's return from a special friend's funeral, I expected the call to be from them to say they had been delayed. A professional yet warm female voice introduced herself as a senior nurse of a Dublin city hospital. I immediately thought of my ongoing back trouble and recent appointments . . . or could it be something to do with great-Aunt Nora's ailing heart? No. Joanna gently explained she was ringing on behalf of Dad to say they had been involved in a car accident. He was concerned I might be worried when they didn't arrive home on time . . . very considerate of him as every extra minute of keeping the boat afloat did require planning and energy.

'But when will they be home?' 'Have they been injured?' My questioning endeavoured to gain some perspective on the situation. Joanna's gentle voice continued to unfold the details: 'Your mother has been injured but your Father is OK'. In a moment of silence an explosion of searching questions erupted in my mind: 'A broken arm needing plastering and then somebody to pick her up in an hour or so? Did I need to come in? Could they still drive the car?' In a struggle to be practical and avoid 'beating around the bush' I found myself posing the ultimate question: 'Look Joanna, I'm a medic myself and I would really appreciate your judgment of the situation so that I can respond accordingly.' Excusing herself briefly to consult the medical team caring for Mum, she soon returned with an updated assessment: 'It is basically like this Lizzy; they are working to resuscitate your mother but . . . but . . . but she's not responding.' Suddenly I found myself despising my medical background. Any hope grounded in ignorance was smashed. 'Oh God, NO!'

As my worst nightmare hit, I became the unsuspecting, frightened bundle being thrust from the warm security of a feathered nest. Not even disbelief and shock cushioned me from the reality of where a nose dive was leading. The long drive into the hospital seemed to stretch into eternity; no amount of struggling could keep me airborne . . . I was plummeting downwards and nothing could stop me. The dank grey drizzle of a mid-November day seemed light in comparison with the black pit I was plunging into. 'So where is your God, now Lizzy?' came the strong accusation from within. I was falling down, down, down, and no amount of neck craning could turn my eyes back up to the heights where I would surely see him. 'OH GOD, WHERE ARE YOU?' – a piercing cry of abandonment from the centre of my being. 'OH GOD OUR HELP IN AGES PAST, OUR HOPE FOR YEARS TO COME!' I found myself spontaneously affirming my faith and trust.

The casualty department waiting-room: an awkward silence as family members congregate . . . a waking nightmare has hit us all. I find my pain and disbelief reflected in each face. My brother Philip maintains a fixed gaze, clutching his lit cigarette; the ash falls unnoticed to the floor. 'Your mother has gone to the operating theatre; please wait. We'll tell you when we have any news.'

I clutch lukewarm coffee in a plastic cup from a vending machine. My other brother, David, gently touches my arm – he arrived before us, just in time to tail the entourage that whipped Mum off for emergency surgery. My heart aches for him, thrown into the whirlpool of such an alien environment. 'The doctor is with your father at present; please wait.'

I fumble in my purse for 10p coins to make a few phone calls; this afternoon's appointments will have to be cancelled. An ambulance brakes at the swing doors, off-loading a patient in the middle of a cardiac arrest – I want to offer my help but my body won't respond. The plastic seats are cold and unyielding, the bin overflowing with empty Coke cans. A television mounted high on the wall is showing a soap opera. The room is full of smoke; the irritation starts me coughing. 'Your father is in X-ray for a spinal scan; please wait.' 'But I thought he was OK!' 'Dislocated knee and hips, a smashed pelvis, shattered upper arm, and gaping wound on his forehead . . . but he *will* be OK. . . . in time.'

I'm afraid to ask the details of the accident for fear there were others injured too. It would be heartbreaking if there were children involved . . . that would surely finish my parents off. And what if it was their fault? Relief! It was only Mum and Dad. A freak accident in which a lorry shed its eight-ton load of timber just at the moment when their car was passing. 'Please God, help the driver!'

The hospital chaplain arrives to escort us to a quieter room; every minute of waiting seems like an hour. We're all locked in our own shock and disbelief unable even to comfort one another. I pull listlessly at a roll of toilet paper in my bag as waves of tears grip me. More phone calls: 'Hello Kaye; Mum and Dad have had a serious car accident – Mum is being operated on this very moment but it's not looking good.' I scarcely believe my own words . . . 'It's not looking good? It's *not* looking good. IT'S NOT LOOKING GOOD!'

In my helplessness I close my eyes and ask God to enfold Mum and Dad in his healing love and to assure them of our love. In the paralysed silence of shock a picture appears:

'It's Mum!' Radiant with a brightness I have never seen before. The dazzling appearance of Christ is reflected in her face! She is gazing into the beautiful face of the one she lived for and loved so much. She is lost in wonder, love and praise . . . '

The cold lifeless shell of a body they say is my mother; the pale frightened face of my father awaiting his place in the operating theatre; the stinging tears held back as he enquires about Mum – with the shock of the accident, a smashed body, overwhelming physical pain and now long hours of anaesthetics to be faced . . . the truth will have to wait until tomorrow.

I am gripped by a need to be strong for Dad and the family but my fate seems sealed. Surely I am finished . . .

> I want no tears when I am gone,
> No useless crying or prayers,
> But a moment of celebration.

These words were written by Mum the evening before she died – challenging words that welcomed a thousand mourners to her farewell service. In our desire to honour her request we did commit ourselves to a moment of celebration – yet we knew she would understand the human frailty of our uncontrollable tears as they broke through from time to time. We were weeping for ourselves and our loss. Yet we truly celebrated where she now found herself. And how often, when life's suffering seemed unbearable, had she found encouragement in her assured final destination!

We laughed momentarily when our rector recalled a conversation between Mum and a good friend on this very subject:

MUM: 'You know Valda, just think, one day you and I will be angels floating on our own individual clouds in heaven. We'll be free of all the pain and suffering of this world. No more lame ducks to look after. No more sleepless nights of worry and pain. Our days will be filled with harp-playing in praise of our Lord as we float along. Just think of it!'

VALDA: 'Yep, I can just imagine it Margaret. I'll be enjoying that OK. But don't you get too excited as I know exactly what you'll be doing . . . propping up everybody else's clouds!'

During those moments of celebration I was given a memorable glimpse of what it was to enter into the fullness of God's presence, to behold his beauty and bathe in the fullness of his healing love – up there in the heights a glimpse of a rejoicing heaven that joined with earth in celebration of Mum's life lived fully for her God.

Huddled at the graveside, burning tears flowing down my face. Eyes fixed on the mahogany coffin lowered to the depths of the vault as ice-cold cutting winds penetrate to the centre of my being. Just at the very moment when I thought for sure I was finished, I found my fall being broken by a big feather cushion. No energy even to question where that cushion came from – just a sigh of relief that I could fall no further. In time I would see that it was a cushion of love and prayers, prayers offered up by so many of God's people. In a state of complete physical, emotional and spiritual shatteredness, I yielded my exhausted body to the softness of its protection and healing. I had landed.

Now the ascent could begin, yet through those early weeks and months it was hard to believe I was on the way up. In the first three months long hours were spent in the car travelling to visit Dad in hospital. As letters of sympathy poured through the letter box we tried to piece together something of our family life . . . without Mum and Dad, without Aunt Nora who had now gone into residential care, without the patter of children's little feet, without the warmth of Mum's kitchen. The hub of family life was no more.

On opening a drawer I discovered my wrapped birthday present, a black turf figure of a mother comforting her distressed, crying child. It was a reminder that not even physical death could drive a wedge into our special bond of love and comfort.

Christmas was survived; cries went out for Mum to take her rightful place once again at the heart of family life. Christmas Eve found me staring into the dark night through the raindrops running down the window pane. A cold, wet, dark and lonely grave seemed so wrong when she could be here in the midst of our warmth and love. We could sit around the log fire together and celebrate the coming of the Christ child.

At new year I found myself back in North Africa for a short visit to pack up my life and work there. Family commitments now calling me back to Dublin left big question marks around my future overseas. Shared tears with special friends helped me to feel, in a tangible way, their showering of love and prayers.

Returning to Dublin affirmed me in my position of 'recuperating passenger'. I relaxed into the security of that love and those prayers. In time I would gain new strength and courage . . . in time.

As my sisters were encouraged to return to college, the tidying away of mum's clothes and belongings was tiptoed through. In my parents' bedroom it seemed appropriate to leave the bedside light on at night as a symbol of hope dispelling our emotional darkness, a light to welcome Dad when he finally returned home, a traumatic and painful road of return until his fragmented and tired body found rest in that big double bed . . . yet now he would occupy it alone.

The softness of my feather cushion continued to hold my grief-stricken body as witnessing my dad's brokenness became unbearable.

With the sun's rising on Easter Sunday I meditated on the first Easter morning sunrise as I placed fresh flowers on Mum's and Anna's graves. The dark pain of Good Friday had truly been lived through during the previous five months. But now the joyful hope of Easter Sunday could be experienced afresh as it became interwoven with that pain. Just as I identified with the grief of the disciples when Jesus was crucified, so now I could appreciate the overwhelming tearful joy of Mary when she arrived at the empty tomb on that first Easter morning. The joy of being told *'He is risen!'*

Sitting on Mum's grave as the dawn cast out the shadows of night's darkness, I knew she had risen with him.

As the upward climb continued I felt ready to begin to stretch my wings, all in the full security of the cushion that still lay firmly underneath.

The first day of summer summoned us to sit on the solid mahogany benches of the Coroner's Court in Dublin. We gathered as a family to hear a blow-by-blow account of the events of 14 November. There were special moments of tearful embracing with the driver of the lorry whose falling load had caused Mum's and Dad's accident. His trembling body and pain-stricken face told his story. The scene brought back painful memories of the accident which had claimed my sister Anna's life five years before. We had sat on those same mahogany benches for an account of *her* untimely death.

The year's progressing brought a return to North Africa into focus. A gentle breeze was lifting my stretched out, exposed wings – so much love, so many prayers willing me on.

Surviving the first anniversary of Mum's and Dad's accident, a surge of strength and mounting courage gripped me. A strong wind was now raising me up – light and airborne.

As my return to North Africa became reality I found myself incapable of not yielding to the strong wind lifting my wings higher and higher. Feelings of excitement, vulnerability and anticipation accompanied my response, all interwoven with the still raw pain of loss and now even more living separation. Despite the assurance that my return overseas was right, strong emotional ties made leaving home traumatic. Witnessing the faith of my dad as he struggled back onto his feet and courageously started piecing together his shattered life, left me full of admiration. A godly force at the centre of his being gave renewed hope and purpose to life. A very special bond of love had grown between us through those months of shared pain and promised healing. I was once again sounding the depths of a growing intimate friendship and its pain of separation.

Feeling the wind of God's spirit blowing between me and my feather cushion I suddenly realized I was flying!

I found myself alone at dawn walking through the deserted town tucked away in the Atlas mountains. Sitting close to the dry river bed awaiting the warmth of the sun's caressing rays, I scanned the cliff face. My longing eyes waited in hopeful anticipation as the shifting shadows of daybreak were dispelled by dazzling orange light. It was then that the eagle took flight! His confidence and maturity after three years flying was striking. Every movement captured my admiration as he soared in the heights and welcomed a new day with a shriek of exhilaration. My spirit became one with him in his flight as I lived in the promise of:

'Those who hope in the Lord will renew their strength; they will soar on wings like eagles. They will run and not grow weary; they will walk and not grow faint!' (Isaiah 40:31 NIV).

Out of tough and painful years had grown an affirmed hope, renewed strength and out-stretched wings. Through growth experienced in the valley the view from the heights was now exhilarating. Yet that exhilaration was mixed with such vulnerability. With the pain of loss and separation still raw and with so much still to learn, at times my wings would surely fail me! Yet a quiet trust assured me of the lasting presence of the feather cushion . . . it would always be there for me.

Reflecting on some words of a song sung by Bette Midler I found expression of my tribute to the one who had always encouraged me to reach for these heights – an earthly mother and best friend who had been such a godly presence in my life.

*Did you ever know that you're my hero,*
*and everything I would hope to be?*
*I can fly higher than an eagle,*
*for you are the wind beneath my wings.*[1]

Larry Henley and Jeff Silbar


You, I thank God for you . . . the wind beneath my wings.
High, high . . . so high I can nearly touch the sky.

Yes, in a very tangible way she had been the wind beneath my wings. And now through the trauma of her passing I was realizing the full capacity of wings stretched out and lifted up by the full force of God's Spirit, which had been the life force at the centre of her being. High, high . . . so high I can nearly touch the sky!

---

[1]  Copyright: Permission sought.

# 12

# Friendship's Heart of Hospitality

The grazing sheep climbed the steep river banks in search of greener pastures, leaving behind the stream which trickled through the middle of this wide and arid North African river bed. Its life-sustaining water encouraged the growth of long green rushes and extended a welcome to those who came there to bathe and drink. And come they did! The loud frog chorus provided audible evidence of those cold-blooded creatures whose camou-flaged skin made it nearly impossible to distinguish them from the dark green reeds and toffee-coloured earth. Year after year their life-cycle continued, as they feasted on procreating mosquitoes' larvae and committed their spawn to the very water from which their sustenance came. They were interrupted only by the spring reappearance of a hungry serpent in search of a tasty morsel – winter's long hibernation had left him ravenous! As the dusk chorus of wallowing frogs gave way to the distinctive buzz of night-time mosquitoes, one could often spot the slithery body of this almost two metre snake returning home to the safety of a deep crevice. Nature's cycle was jealously protected in this place of stark beauty seldom disturbed by human presence.

Sheep drank at the stream before ascending to the rolling hills covered in lush spring growth. Good winter rains had turned these rugged caramel foothills into an explosion of wild flowers, and the grass, toughened by exposure to the harsh climate, was now dotted with fiery red poppies, and ready to be feasted on.

Resting in the foothills, and surrounded by this carpet of pasture, a cluster of palm trees stretched high into the clear blue sky enjoying welcome rays of spring sunshine. Once laden with winter's mouth-watering dates, the elegant palms now rejoiced in a newfound freedom to rustle in the breeze. And what a shady haven they provided for an afternoon siesta! Cold nights and warm days were characteristic of spring weather. The setting was idyllic – a background of foothills adorned by pine trees oozing fragrant sap and weighed down with pregnant cones. The soft, distinctive crackle of their opening increased in volume as the warmth of the day encouraged the 'aeroplane' seeds into flight, the wind lifting them high and carrying them to fertile soil where their life cycle would continue.

It was a joy to be sharing the delights of this place on Easter Sunday with a North African Muslim friend. Safia and I had become good friends over the previous two years, enjoying hospitality of heart and mind. Her skills as a language teacher were much appreciated as I struggled to get my mouth and throat around the guttural Arabic language. There had been many laughs as she guided me through the disappointment of stupid language blunders. One of my early assignments had been to purchase the ingredients for a date cake, make it and enjoy eating it together. With a head full of new words I set off for the local shops in search of the necessary. My first stop found me confidently asking for two packets of rubbish instead of butter (the subtle difference between *zibla* and *zibda*). The intrigued shop owner asked what I was going to do with the rubbish. Hearing I was to make a cake left him musing on the 'West's' recycling of paper taken to the creative extreme! He declined an offer to taste the final product.

Safia was always there to pick me up when cultural and linguistic misunderstandings threatened to drive me into a pit of despair. Telling anaemic pregnant women to eat a car twice a day (instead of an iron tablet!) could have had drastic effects. Oh, those long hours of working on pronunciation as I endeavoured to sound the difference between *karhba* and *kaahba*! No appreciable decrease in car numbers reassured me that the women had probably come to the conclusion I was just a 'wacky' foreigner with weird ideas about treating anaemia – as well as about making cakes! I often wondered if I would *ever* master this language . . . but Safia was always there encouraging me on. 'One day, Lizzy; one day, Lizzy!' One day!

Drawn from very different backgrounds, languages, cultures and religions, we had so much to offer to and receive from each other. Commitment in friendship drew us together and led us on a journey that promised to enrich our lives. Hospitality marked the Amri family who always invited me to share in special celebrations. Open hearts and an open home offered me a sincere welcome among them when I found myself far from my own family. Their warmth and concern was genuine and touched me deeply.

Safia's father, Mohammed Amri, was a devout Muslim dedicated to his family and position as director of the local school. His reputation as a skilled teacher of Arabic caused parents from all over the town to find a way to ensure a place for their children in his class. On late summer afternoons little groups of neatly-dressed children wearing skull caps would sit cross-legged on the verandah for extra tuition. Mini-blackboards in hand, they drew lines and curves in white chalk . . . listening intently to the instructions of their respected teacher. He was held in high regard by the community and many came to him seeking counsel and advice. His wisdom in accepting an arranged marriage to his first cousin Jamila led to years of shared happiness. He was openly proud of his three sons and two daughters, who were all encouraged to study hard and make something of themselves. Through them the honoured family name and reputation would be carried on.

As the eldest child, Safia followed proudly in her father's footsteps and trained as a teacher. Salwa (the second eldest) dreamed of being a doctor. Samir, the eldest boy, left home to study in a neighbouring country. In time he would return qualified in computer technology and take his place as man of the house. Samir took seriously his unspoken (yet well understood) role of ensuring that the family honour was preserved. This meant a special focus on Safia and Salwa – watching their every move and imposing strict rules concerning their contact with men outside the family. Yet he need not have worried as both girls held their father in high regard and committed themselves to maintaining high moral standards. The honour of the Amri family would not be marred by their conduct. By all accounts happiness and harmony radiated through the hospitality of this family. 'Allah has looked down upon us with favour!' were words often uttered by their mother.

Jamila was a wonderful example of a North African woman's commitment to home and family. Her waking moments were filled with endless cleaning, cooking, washing and the rearing of five children . . . especially pampering the male members of the family! With summer knocking at our door, her long hours working at the loom became more urgent . . . she assured me that clippers (like those I used on my 'loo-brush' hairstyle!) would soon be in use again. In a matter of days these grazing sheep's woolly winter coats would be shorn, leaving them light and free. The delicate and important job of washing, drying, dying, spinning and weaving their wool into precious blankets was a woman's laborious task. Watching Safia's mum left me with no illusions about how long and tiring the process was. Yet it was so rewarding to see the final product in place . . . no duvets needed here!

Sheep, sheep, sheep! So much part of North African culture. Highly valued and appreciated not only for their wool but also for their meat. Each one was destined ultimately for slaughter. And when that day came they would lie in silence and acceptance awaiting their end. With the utterance of the name of Allah a knife would be put to their throats and the life blood left to drain from their bodies. With the removal of the skin, precious meat would be divided up for cooking . . . nothing wasted.

Climbing the hill with Safia and seeing these woolly animals grazing took my mind back to the celebration of the Muslim festival of Eid ul Adha – the feast of sacrifice. Early in the morning of that festival each Muslim household would sacrifice a sheep in remembrance of the sacrifice Abraham had made in place of his son Ishmael. Throughout the day meat would be shared with those who came to visit.

The previous Eid I had arrived mid-morning to spend the day with Safia's family. It seemed the most appropriate place to be on this occasion. Safia's father expected me to be there, despite the lack of formal invitation, and was somewhat put out that I hadn't arrived earlier! Relieved to have missed the slaughtering of the sheep I apologized profusely for my late arrival. It touched me that he felt his family was incomplete without my presence. I never ceased to be amazed by such a display of protective care. I was their adopted daughter for as long as my life and work lay in North Africa and away from my own family in Ireland. I was living in a culture which nursed such a strong sense of belonging to a family that in many respects my friendships were strangely incomplete until the fuller picture of where I had come from as a person could be shared. How Safia's family longed for the day when they could meet my parents!

Sitting with Safia that evening of Eid ul Adha, friendship's hospitality of heart and mind allowed us to share a great story of God's faithful provision. The story of Abraham's sacrifice appears in both the Koran and the Bible – with some differences! Huddled together in front of a fragrant incense-burning charcoal fire, I listened to her story of how Abraham was prepared to sacrifice Ishmael. With the background hum of a teapot brewing on the hot coals, we then read together the biblical version of how Abraham took a sharp knife to the neck of his son Isaac. Yet God provided a lamb to be offered in his place. What Abraham was asked to do he had done, by offering his only son.

'So sheep are very much part of biblical culture too!' Safia exclaimed in amazement. Out of that evening came the opportunity to explore together their place in Old Testament sacrifice. My new appreciation of the cultural setting 'fine-tuned' my senses in a way I had never experienced before. So it was with a great sense of adventure that we set out on this road of exploration. Reading with eyes and ears wide open, praying that God would satisfy our desire to know more . . . I knew we wouldn't be disappointed.

Soon we were uncovering one of the most beautiful jewels among God's treasures. As a diamond has many facets, so this jewel of atonement has facets that reflect and radiate the glory of a compassionate and loving God. And how special it was to be unveiling that jewel with a Muslim friend who had such an appreciation of offering a blood sacrifice! Yet as rivers of blood poured out across the Muslim world on the day of Eid ul Adha, Safia noted a marked absence of blood sacrifice in Christianity today. 'So what has happened between the many blood sacrifices of the Old Testament and now?' She demanded. Our journey of discovery continued.

That particular Easter Sunday was also celebrated with my parents who had come to visit me in North Africa. Their excitement at meeting them in person was reflected in the exceptional hospitality offered by Safia's family. Traditional North African couscous was served, followed by abundant dates and oranges for dessert. In return it was our treat to invite Safia to join us on our Easter outing. We had chosen this secluded mountainous spot for an afternoon walk to be followed by a picnic of barbecued lamb. We could buy the meat from a roadside butcher who displayed the head and feet of today's slaughter outside his shop. When we had chosen the cut of meat we wanted he would set it to barbecue over red-hot coals. The meat would then be served with (fairly) fresh bread and red pepper paste doused in olive oil, all washed down with a bottle of Coke. Burp, belch! What a contrast to the traditional New Zealand lamb served with roast potatoes, steamed vegetables and mint sauce which normally graced an Irish Easter Sunday lunch table!

This culture's open slaughtering of animals did nothing for Mum's appetite. I did my best to keep her mind off the subject as we tucked into our picnic. The laughter and chat were soon disturbed however, when a pickup truck offloaded the lamb destined for tomorrow's chop. Disbelief at our visitor's unfortunate timing left me assuring Mum he was just 'in transit'. Tied with the sleeve of a jumper to the pole next to Mum, this lonely soul read compassion on her face and started bleating as if in petition for his life. 'Lizzy, I think he's thirsty; please ask someone to give him a drink.' Mum's pleading look compelled me to relay the request to the butcher. Both he and I knew the lamb was bleating from loneliness and the desire to be close to his mother, but I certainly wasn't going to tell my mum that! Allowing her to think he was thirsty seemed by far the kindest option. The butcher laughed at mum's sensitivity but kindly placed a bucket of water in front of the sheep. Baa, Baa! The lamb's gazing at Mum was now punctuated with glances at the bucket! Ah well, it was worth a try.

In contrast to Mum's concern, Dad's excitement bubbled over as he assisted the butcher at the barbecue. A delicious aroma wafted up with pillars of smoke from the sizzling grill. Round two of our picnic was on its way. Despite not having a word of Arabic, Dad was 'chuffed' at his apparent ability to communicate by non-verbal means. He happily took photos of the scene ignoring Mum's obvious unease with it all. The 'go ahead' was given to photograph the lamb which suddenly fell silent as the butcher insisted on posing himself straddled across its back. Just as Dad focused his camera to record this harmless scene, a huge knife appeared from the butcher's pocket and the lamb's throat was cut. Cheers! The blood drained from Mum's face as quickly as it did from the lamb's neck. As she keeled over Dad's excitement waned dramatically – despite the butcher's grinning from ear to ear. Surely the whole point of asking to take a photo was to register this exciting moment? I had a nasty feeling that the entertainment would not be included in the overall price of the barbecue. Insult waited to be added to injury when it was time to produce a tip. The party fell decidedly flat. Safia wasn't quite sure how to react but very kindly revived Mum with water drawn from the bucket. Oh, the joys of sharing in each other's families . . .

As we travelled home, the words of a song we had sung during our Easter morning celebrations came to mind.

> Led like a lamb to the slaughter
> in silence and shame,
> there on Your back You carried
> a world of violence and pain.
> Bleeding, dying, bleeding, dying.
>
> Graham Kendrick[1]

---

[1]  Extract taken from the song 'Led Like A Lamb to the Slaughter' by Graham Kendrick, Copyright © 1983 Kingsway's Thankyou Music, PO Box 5, Eastbourne, East Sussex BN23 6NW, UK. Used by kind permission of Kingsway's Thankyou Music.

Suddenly snippets of the Easter story came alive in the whole drama of what had been planned as a fun picnic. A helpless lamb tied and destined for slaughter – a picture of Jesus being led to the cross for crucifixion. And then there were the different reactions of those who looked on:

– My mum, who couldn't handle the cruelty so tried hard to believe it wouldn't happen. Her distress and nausea at the deliberate act of slaughter painted a picture of Mary (the mother of Jesus) and Jesus' close friends. As they watched him being nailed to the cross they were overwhelmed by emotion.

– Then there was my dad, who was initially taken in by the excitement of it all, but came crashing down to earth at the sight of blood and what it signified. Death! How many people were drawn unthinkingly into the enthusiasm of the crowd around Jesus, crying 'Crucify him; crucify him!' Yet sober reality hit when the whole land was covered by darkness and Jesus breathed his last. Their thoughts may have echoed the voice of the Roman centurion who, seeing what happened, exclaimed, 'Surely this was a righteous man!'

– And finally there was the butcher who took it all in his stride. Maybe that was a picture of the soldiers for whom the crucifixion was routine. Hammering nails into human flesh was just another day's work. As they sat at the foot of the cross casting lots for Jesus' clothes, they offered him wine vinegar to drink. But that was no comfort to him.

Out of this scene came a contextualized response to Safia's question concerning the lack of blood sacrifice in Christianity today. Jesus the perfect 'lamb' of God was offered as the one complete atoning sacrifice. His crucifixion and death marked the abolition of Old Testament sacrifice. I'm sure lots of sheep were happy about that!

Some weeks later, whilst enjoying an Indian meal I had prepared, Safia announced that she was accepting an offer of a contract to work as a teacher in Oman. My heart sank . . . I was going to miss her terribly. She assured me it would only be for a year to gain experience and some extra money. Somebody needed to pay for

Samir's education which was turning out to be more expensive than previously estimated. I immediately wondered how she would cope outside a family unit that provided so much support. How often we had shared the difficulties of maintaining the status of a single person in a society that looks upon you as only half a woman if you don't marry and have children. If struggling with singleness in North African culture was not easy, then it would be ten times more difficult in such a conservative Islamic culture as Oman far away from home. As a Christian I could find fulfilment in my singleness but that just wasn't an option for a North African Muslim girl. I braced myself for the goodbye that lay on the horizon.

It was a warm summer's morning when the long-awaited phone call came through to the Amri family residence. After six years of hard medical studies Safia's sister Salwa was now a fully qualified doctor. A sheep grazing in their garden was to be slaughtered to mark the occasion. A big party would be thrown to celebrate both her success and her engagement to Toufiq which could now go ahead. Five long years of patient waiting on Toufiq's part would now be rewarded as his intention to marry Salwa was sealed. As Salwa ecstatically absorbed the details of her achievement, Safia ran bursting with excitement to break the news to her father who was taking a morning rest. As her words poured out she gently shook his frail frame to awaken him. 'Father, father, wake up. Salwa's a doctor!' But his lifeless body failed to respond. She now found herself shaking him forcefully and raising her voice, 'Father, father, you *must* wake up. Salwa's a doctor!' With repetition the words became louder and turned from a command to a desperate plea. Still no response. A cry to Salwa left the telephone receiver thrown to one side. Salwa now found herself pathetically trying to instil life-giving breath into her father's still warm body. But his tired spent heart could not be coaxed back into beating – its day of rest had come.

Having gasped his last as the phone rang, Safia's father would never know that his daughter, of whom he was so proud, was now a doctor. From the heights of elation to the depths of sorrow . . .

the fall couldn't have been any longer and sharper! 'Yes, Salwa is a doctor, but Baba is dead.'

As shocked family and friends congregated to express their sympathy the Imam from the mosque was called to chant verses from the Koran. Mohammed Amri's body was wrapped in white cloth and buried by the menfolk before sunset. The verandah where I had sat with him only two evenings before was now crowded with weeping women. The background drumming of 'Allah Akbar!' (God is great) pierced the night sky and would continue to do so over the next forty days until the deceased's spirit was laid to rest.

On returning from the graveyard the male folk joined the dazed gathering. Few words were exchanged – soft weeping and the chant of the Imam said it all. As the evening closed in some people took their leave and others shared in a meal. Before returning home the Imam called the immediate family together to offer special prayers for Safia's father. Retiring to the stillness of the sitting-room, Jamila and her children waited in silence for this respected religious authority to lead them in prayer. At that moment Safia found me on the overcrowded verandah. Gently she took my hand and through eyes overflowing with grief pleaded, 'Come, Lizzy!' No words were necessary as the understanding was there. Having prayed when we read the Bible together, she was now asking for my hospitality of heart to be there with her in the spiritual depth of this moment. Vulnerability cried out to be held tight in friendship's bond of love. As those present sat with hands cupped in prayer, the despair and lostness of the moment struck hard. As the Imam pleaded with 'Allah the most merciful' my thoughts went back to our Easter Sunday picnic. The imagery of the slaughtered lamb told only part of the story. The song we had sung on Easter morning had other verses too, verses bearing words of life and hope.

> At the right hand of the Father
> now seated on high,
> You have begun Your eternal
> reign of justice and joy.

*You're alive,*
*You're alive*
*You have risen,*
*Alleluia!*
*And the power*
*and the glory*
*is given,*
*Alleluia!*
*Jesus to You.*

Graham Kendrick[2]

Through my cupped hands I prayed, 'Jesus, to you', the facets of whose atoning life reflected and radiated the glory of a compassionate and loving God.

The completion of forty days of mourning was marked by a special religious ceremony. On that day it was the family's deepest desire that Mohammed Amri's spirit would be 'laid to rest'. Since his death, hours, days and weeks of petitioning before Allah had endeavoured to ensure a place of eternal rest for Mohammed's wandering spirit. Now it depended on the mercy of Allah and his graciousness on this day of decision. As of this day the family could once again move freely in the community, remove their mourning clothes and watch television. It was also the painful day before Safia's departure for Oman. A signed contract meant losing too much if she backed out at this stage. So the day was marked by the slaughtering of a sheep – the sheep which was to have been used to celebrate Salwa's graduation and engagement. What a day!

Two years later Safia and I returned to sit once more at the edge of this North African river bed. Drinking in the beauty of an unchanging environment we were acutely aware of the many changes that had occurred in both our lives in the years since we had last sat in this place. We laughed as we remembered our Easter

---

[2]   Extract taken from the song 'Led Like A Lamb to the Slaughter' by Graham Kendrick, Copyright © 1983 Kingsway's Thankyou Music, PO Box 5, Eastbourne, East Sussex BN23 6NW, UK. Used by kind permission of Kingsway's Thankyou Music.

picnic with Mum and Dad. We shed tears as the pain and grief of losing Safia's father returned to us. What an experience that had been of sounding the depths of sorrow together and finding God was there! With my return to Ireland on leave had come Safia's departure for Oman. Those early days of living separation were hard as, still wrapped in the dark shawl of bereavement, she faced such a lonely existence. Promises to return home after a year melted with the reawakening of a romance in her life, a romance that would lead to marriage in only a matter of days from now. And what then? She and Ahmed would make Oman their home. If their firstborn was a son they would name him Mohammed after her father.

With the laughter that accompanied our Easter Sunday walk still ringing in our ears it was hard to talk about the loss and grief in my own life since we had last shared moments in this oasis of beauty – loss and grief that had come through a car accident which had cost my mum her life and left my dad physically and emotionally smashed up. Our picnic seemed like only yesterday – sheep still grazing, palm branches rustling in the wind, frogs croaking and the same snake hawking. The butcher still asked after my parents and for copies of the photographs my dad took! Yet my increased grey hairs and eyes pregnant with pain were telltale reminders of what I had been through since that day.

In just a week our ways would divide once more and only God knew when they would cross again. I reflected on the path along which our friendship had brought us in these last five years. True hospitality of heart and mind had allowed us to laugh together as we shared in each other's joys . . . and how we had laughed! We had also known what it was to empathize in life's struggles as the other's became our own. A burden shared was truly a burden halved. It was a hospitality of heart which gave us the freedom to weep with each other when the pain of life's experience threatened to overwhelm us, tears that continued to be shed across the miles and expressed in a simple card that said, 'I love you, dear friend, and weep with you in the loss of your mother.'

It was a hospitality that left us pondering on the richness of a God-given friendship, a friendship that refused to be limited by differences in culture, language or religion. Actually in some strange way its richness lay in those very differences. It was a friendship that promised to span the boundaries of continent, time and life's progressing, a friendship in which we would always seek the best for each other, confident in the experience of:

> *When I lift you,*
> *my friend,*
> *my arms grow stronger.*
> *When I give to you,*
> *my hand empties to receive.*
> *When I walk with you through*
> *dark valleys,*
> *my feet gain experience.*
> *When I weep with you,*
> *my eyes wash clear to see*
> *compassion's holy bond.*
> *When I lift you,*
> *I am lifted.*

Susan L. Lenzkes[3]

---

[3] From 'A Silver Pen for Cloudy Days' by Susan L. Lenzkes, copyright © 1986 by Susan L. Lenzkes. Permission requested.

# 13

# Duet Playing

The sharp wind of a freezing December night blew in my face as I hurried along the dark narrow streets. Empty crisp bags, chocolate wrappers and newspapers joined the last of autumn's leaves swirling around my ankles. From street lamp to street lamp I dodged in haste, shielded from the full force of the gale by a scarf, woolly hat, gloves, thick leather boots and a long coat. Clutching my violin case in one hand I kept my head down, only looking up occasionally to verify my bearings. Despite all this my face was numb and my fingers like frozen sausages inside my gloves. It must have been the coldest night of that British winter.

The winter months preceded a return to my life and work as a midwife in North Africa following an unexpected year at home in Ireland, a year during which the deep pain and shock of my parents' accident and my mother's death had been lived through, my badly injured dad had been nursed back onto his feet, the shattered fragments of family life had been pieced together, and the hard reality of living separation from Mum had been faced. It was also a year during which music had become a very important part of my life – ministering deeply to my broken heart. Many hours had been poured into discovering the depths of my seasoned violin. Now I was engaged in further cross-cultural studies in England as I found myself 'in transit' from Ireland to North Africa.

By any reckoning it had been an emotionally chilling year for me and somehow the piercing physical cold of this evening was not unfamiliar. Yet my heart was warm with excitement, if somewhat nervous, at the thought of the hours which lay ahead. Excitement because spending time with a gifted musician not only inspired me but also taught me so much. Yet my nervousness showed in the awkward fumbling of my fingers on the strings, uncontrollable bouncing bow, inability to count, stiff vibrato, and haphazard interpretation. How I longed to become one with my instrument and play it to its full potential!

My thoughts went back to the first time I had stepped in from the cold into the small terraced home of this remarkable teacher. Wow! One foot over the threshold of an uninspiring door, no different from the 80 others along that street, and I found myself in another world. Numb from the cold and rendered speechless by the environment, I stood in wide-eyed amazement soaking in my surroundings. A baby grand piano filled a third of the room with violins and bows of varying shapes and sizes resting on its open top. A tiny violin caught my eye, causing me to muse: 'That's the size a four-year-old Wolfgang Amadeus Mozart would have used to play "Twinkle, twinkle little star".' The oak beams supported bookshelves of music, music and more music. A casually placed spotlight caught the outline of a bronze bust of Ludwig Van Beethoven in a corner, above music stands, instrument cases, fallen manuscripts and a cat sleeping on a pile of clean washing in a Moses basket! A peep under the piano revealed the storage niche for an electric violin/viola and electric cello – along with the amplifiers and leads necessary to bring them to life. This guy was into jazz as well as the great classics!

Sketches of famous musicians adorned any available wall and door space, while soft lighting gave a special warmth and cosiness to the setting. Yet 'warm and cosy' were not words I would have used to describe the physical temperatures – excessive heat not being good for wooden instruments and cosiness decidedly bad for the concentration. Nor were they words appropriate to describe the hours I would spend in that room pursuing my heart's desire: to transform playing an instrument into playing music. 'I have come to learn how to play music' – a simple explanation of the sincere quest which brought me to that place on such a wintry night. 'I have heard that you are an outstanding musician and teacher. My time here is short but I'm committed to learning as much as I can and giving it my best. Will you please take me on?' A teacher knows a keen pupil: one with a clear goal before him and committed to the hard slog. In such a case it is a delight to be able to respond with a positive 'Yes'.

And so, for those months, braving winter's unrelenting elements was no hardship as I edged my way nearer my desired goal. Soon my admired and trusted teacher invited me to play duets with him. Still incredulous at the proposition – he was a born optimist, obviously keen to stretch me to the limit – I watched as he reached up to one of the many shelves and extracted a well-worn manuscript. On these yellowing dog-eared pages was a duet for violins written some centuries earlier – I had never heard of the composer before.

I felt incredibly unworthy to be playing with such a musician. Yet there was no hiding from the reality of my inexperience as his wisdom and discernment left me bare before him. He knew better than anyone my grade, my clumsiness, and my weaknesses. Yet he had eyes to see beyond those to a potential known only to him, a potential interwoven with my ever-growing desire to touch the heart of music. If this was the informed context in which the invitation was extended then I was willing to trust him and respond with an acceptance. 'I'll give it a go but I can't promise anything!'

And so the painful journey of attaining harmony and transforming notes into music began. And was that journey painful! Through the agony of it all I found encouragement in a poster adorning the wall before me which expressed the sentiments of Johann Sebastian Bach:

I PLAY THE NOTES AS THEY ARE WRITTEN
BUT IT IS GOD WHO MAKES THE MUSIC

The first thing I discovered was that I lacked the confidence to come in on the right note, a problem further exacerbated by my inability to keep count – causing me to drop out when we did get

started . . . discovery number two! 'Keep going Lizzy, keep going
. . . don't stop!' came a vain plea of encouragement from the first
violin taking the lead and playing on beautifully. And so we would
start again and again and again! Truly I marvelled at this teacher's
patience and persistence! He had an incredible belief that I could
make it – doing his best to help me by tapping his foot on the floor
and even rapping me on the shoulder with his bow! I wouldn't have
blamed him for clonking me on the head out of sheer frustration!
But long-suffering perseverance was at the core of his character. I
was happy he believed in me – being at pains to believe in myself.
His outstanding playing helped hold the tune and covered a
multitude of my fumblings. As I gained in confidence he would
draw more out of me, with the tune passing from the first violin
to the second and back to the first violin again. The music, written
for two instruments, was strikingly incomplete when only one
violin played. There was no 'opting out' allowed here!

The tune carried us through a light hearted 'Allegro' on to a paced 'Andante', slow 'Largo' and 'Lento largo' as the lament of a breaking heart gradually unfolded. My counting was getting better – the weeks of tension headaches, frustration, sweat and tears were paying off. Although playing the right notes in tune and at the right moment had soaked up my concentration and energy, it was now time to add feeling and expression.

On one of those cold winter evenings my hour's lesson focused on three short bars of music. They were crucial bars that held the heart of the lament and in the muted light of this inspiring room, my patient teacher was determined to transform my playing. The air had been charged with his mission from the very moment I stepped through the door. Yet such was the intensity of the occasion that I came the closest I have ever come to 'packing it in'. Notes, counting and expression were a lot to concentrate on all at once . . . my fingers and arms ached, my neck and shoulders tensed up in response to all the stress, my eyes strained to keep up with the music and my head felt as if it was going to blow up at any moment. Yet we had come so far that turning back was no longer an option. We would get there . . . eventually! 'Just listen, Lizzy, to what I'm playing and allow your part to slip into place.'

It must have been in the last moments of our evening lesson, when I had given up all hope of getting my brain around the task before me, that something amazing happened. We were playing those three bars for the umpteenth time when SUDDENLY all we had been striving for came together!

For the first time the heart of the lament was truly heard. I stopped playing and stood in dazed silence. 'Did you hear that, Lizzy? Did you hear it?' came the excited questioning of my teacher. 'Yes, yes, I heard it all right!' – was my enthusiastic response. 'What was it? What happened?' – the questioning continued. 'Emm, something happened but I'm not really sure what. There was some kind of a transformation.' I fumbled trying to put it into words. 'You've got it! You've got it!' he exclaimed, 'The two violins became one – a transformation that lifted the tune from plain manuscript to true music – a transformation that will carry it deep into the hearts of others.' *Wow*, Now that is what I call playing music!

At the end of my lesson that evening when I was all wrapped up ready to brave winter's elements once again, my teacher stopped me at the door and poured out his desire to know something more of my life and work overseas. It was a topic we had only touched on before, leaving me feeling it wasn't of any particular interest to him. How wrong I was! 'Tell me, Lizzy, how do you respond to such an ocean of need in your life and work in North Africa?' he inquired. 'For me, music is an incredible extravagance when there is such pain and suffering all around us. OK, I've been to Romania and set up a trust for an orphanage out there. I've driven lorries of food and clothes out to the children in an effort to express my care. But it's not enough – the sense of guilt remains every time I pick up my violin and play. I really admire what you're doing!'

Admire what I'm doing! . . . I respected and admired him all the more. His confrontation had caught me totally off guard. He was right – music WAS an extravagance if detached from the heartthrob of human existence. For in as much as music was now on my mind, the gnawing guilt of an inadequate response to a hurting world was sincerely on his.

I replied slowly. 'But if we can discover how God feels for our hurting society, his empowerment will make a lasting difference. Come to think of it, it's rather like duet-playing! For the master musician's heart breaks when he sees us stamp, squeeze, wring and blast life from each other and he extends an invitation to join his lament. But playing the second violin isn't easy. It's hard to know where to begin. Just as the effort poured into controlling a bow can produce muscle spasm, so the pain of disappointment and apparent fruitless investment promises to grip you from time to time. "Oh, God, help me to trust you for enduring strength!" Yet with the goal of attaining harmony and sounding the true depths of the music ever before you, you "hang in there".

'In that moment of "arriving" all the pain and struggle will be more than worthwhile. No longer will two violins be heard for they will have become one in purpose and unity . . . the playing of a deep and moving tune full of expression. A powerful, transforming lament now working through you to touch the lives of others. Now THAT is what makes the difference!!'

Braving the cutting winds of that bitter December night, I became acutely aware of the important interweaving of music in my life and work. The raw pain of biting frost became a reminder of the pain of so many who had passed though the 'curtain of separation': Tahir's weeping mother clutching a plastic medal; Lai's gentle hands massaging Dang's limp frame; Mohammed's snapped cord; the bodies of Wahiba and her son being carried out for burial under cover of darkness; Rachida's 'bay window' eyes pregnant with pain as she remounted a camel and rode into the setting sun; Anna's rose-clad coffin; Karima's search for diamonds in the dust of her earthly existence; Nabiha and Yasmin's beautiful bond of love so brutally shattered; Habiba's joy at 'three for the price of one' which later became the sacrifice of 'one for the price of three'; my precious mother and friend whose sudden death plummeted me to within a feather of destruction on sharp boulders – only to mount up on eagles' wings and learn how to soar. Finally Safia's heart of hospitality which allowed us to share in each other's joys, struggles and pains . . . a friendship which makes it all worthwhile!

Through sharing in each of these lives I had been able to hear more clearly in my heart the lament of the master musician and respond unconditionally to the invitation to play second violin. I have given it my best, I have given it my life, and I have tasted the delights of attained harmony.

It starts with heartfelt searching . . . leading to an open door:

'I HAVE COME TO LEARN HOW TO PLAY MUSIC.
WILL YOU PLEASE TAKE ME ON?'

BUT WE HAVE THIS TREASURE IN JARS OF CLAY
TO SHOW THAT THIS ALL-SURPASSING POWER
IS FROM GOD AND NOT US.

2 CORINTHIANS 4:7. (NIV)

# Questions for Individual Reflection and Group Discussion

This section has been compiled, on request, by my highly respected tutor Chris Wright of All Nations Christian College, where I had the privilege of studying some years ago in preparation for a cross-cultural life and work. In the context of our tutor group we read and discussed, under Chris's guidance and thought-provoking questions, case studies similar to the stories I have brought together in this collection. So valuable were those sessions that many of the issues raised have stayed with me until this day. Through this discussion section my desire is to provide readers with an opportunity to use my stories in a similar way, if they so wish. I firmly believe that 'two heads are better than one' when it comes to certain issues, so would encourage the use of these questions in a group setting as well as for individual reflection. It always proved helpful to come to the discussion having read the story and the relevant questions beforehand.

The fact that I am a committed Christian means that a few of the questions (or certain parts of them) may prove relevant only to those who share the same persuasion. Yet my faith does not remove me from being human – far from it! Most of these questions are written from a very human standpoint, rendering them valuable for use by a wide range of people, both Christian and non-Christian.

For those who seek to respond more fully to our world in need; for those in training to work in a cross-cultural situation; for those who desire to understand and support in a deeper way the many who have already given themselves to this life and work overseas . . . this section is for you.

## Gunpowder: the Fragrance of Death

1) Ahmed reckoned that Allah had been good to him by causing him to lose a leg and thus avoid losing his life in the war. How would you respond to this attempt to rationalize and bring some good purpose out of suffering? Would a 'Western' and/or Christian response have been any different?

2) What can you say, then, to the converse fact that Tahir, who seemed less badly injured initially, was spared only to return to the battle and lose his life altogether? Do questions of the goodness and purposes of God become pointless in the face of suffering so blatantly caused by human evil, violence and greed?

3) Would the story have had any different complexion if the boys and the mother of Tahir had been Christians, or citizens of a 'Christian country' at war with another? If so, in what way? If not, what implications does that have for penetrating the depth of human misery and heroism and the way it transcends cultural and religious differences?

4) Are there any ways in which medical or aid workers can be prepared for the conditions and strains of working, like Lizzy, in a war-zone? How important is a sense of humour, glimpses of which shine through the pain of this story?

## With the Flick of a Switch

1) Is there any difference in this story related to the Buddhist faith of the suffering parents, as distinct from the predominant Islamic context of most of the other stories?

2) Lizzy found a point of contact and sympathy by relating her own Irish identity and history to that of the young Vietnamese couple and their plight. How important is it to find such links between our own culture and that of those we serve? What dangers would there be in superficial comparisons? How could such links prove helpful as bridges to sharing the heart of Lizzy's Christian faith?

## Snapped Cords

1) Should Lizzy have attempted more forcefully to overrule Fatma's 'solution' to the trapped cord and do the job 'properly' and thus avoid the potential fatality when the cord snapped? It might have been a life-and-death decision, yet cultural sensitivity and being rebuffed as an 'outsider' compelled Lizzy to give way to the traditional birth-attendant. How do you assess that?

2) Language mistakes are an inevitable and accepted part of the stress of living in a different culture. Usually they are harmless and humorous. But in this case, Kaltouma's misunderstanding was very denting to Lizzy's professional confidence, her desire to be an expression of God's care, as well as her struggle to learn the language in the first place. Was she right just to accept it, learn from the blunder, and try to cope with it by self-laughter despite the pain of disappointment? Would it have helped, or made things worse, to try to explain the mistake to Kaltouma in an attempt to salvage some of her reputation?

## A Healthy Child is a Picture of God, a Hurting Child of his Son

1) How would you cope with the loss of health and/or life for reasons of cultural choice and tradition when a western medical/charitable option was available that could have made a difference?

2) What lesson can be learnt from the experience of Helga and Ben and the consequences? Western 'success' was paid for at the cost of loss of cultural identity, and probably ultimately by the loss of life itself (which might, of course, have happened earlier anyway). What might you have said to Helga: a) before her decision to 'save' Ben? b) after the prolonged 'silence' which seemed to indicate that he had perished?

3) What criteria would help to distinguish between beneficial and constructive western aid on the one hand and counter-productive and potentially destructive (though well-meant) interference on the other?

4) Lizzy was helped to cope with the tragedy of the transformation of a healthy child into a suffering and dying one by reflection on the Bible's twin portrayal of God as the creating Father and as the suffering, rejected, dying Son. Was that an appropriate 'earthing' of her Christian theology? In what other contexts would such an insight be helpful? Would there be any way of communicating to a Muslim the comfort that such reflection brought her, in view of an absent theology of a 'suffering God' in Islam?

## All Sunshine Makes a Desert

1) In what sense, if all, is it right to read this as a story of 'failure'.

2) How do you account for Malika's combined expression of acceptance of Allah's 'victory', and gratitude to Lizzy? What did it teach Lizzy about herself, her God and her charge?

3) In cold statistics, it was just a fifth still-birth. Lizzy's help in pregnancy and at the delivery made no difference. Or did it? In what ways would Malika have been transformed by Lizzy's 'Christ-like compassion, unveiled face, and God-given love'?

4) Can we learn true humility only through shattering professional or personal failure, or impotence? It may be easy to say yes, but who pays the cost when others are involved? Or is this another insight into the way God can bring healing through loss and death?

## A Frog with a Sore Throat

1) Many kinds of Christian and non-Christian mission seem to think that short-term 'in and out' forays are sufficient. How do you weigh them against Lizzy's determination to sweat through the hard work of language learning and cultural immersion? Could she have been any use to the people of the culture in which she wanted to work (especially to 'the poor, powerless and pregnant'), if she had not taken time to stand, to listen, to smell and to see?

2) What implications does your response to the above question have to the need and nature of training for cross-cultural life and work?

## Love's Price Tag

1) What might you have said to the cleaner in response to her comments about Nabiha, and their implication that her situation was somehow her own fault?

2) Lizzy speaks several times of her anger in the situation, and her attempt to use it constructively. In what circumstances is anger proper and acceptable, and how can one use it positively? What potential traps might Lizzy's anger have led her into culturally, professionally, or spiritually if she had not controlled it?

3) The story starkly points out the tension of being 'affluent' in knowledge, skills and resources, and yet 'impotent' because of the cultural barriers. How can one prepare to cope with such tension? Should Lizzy have tried to do anything to prevent the separation and the fate of Yasmin? If so, what?

4) Another ironic tension in the story is the fact that Lizzy was only present in the situation because of her professional skills, training and compassion which were needed. Yet in another sense, at the point of crisis, she was not needed and not really welcome. ('My Western "power" fell outside the boundaries of this culture . . . The distinct lack of invitation at that

moment was marked'). Is it worth submitting to such tearing apart? Another Christian worker in a different context was once told by those he was working among, 'You are needed here, but not wanted.' Is it possible to work/serve in such an atmosphere?

5) Was all the joy and positive progress of the bonding weeks of any ultimate value in itself, given the final separation of mother and child and its probable consequences? In what way would Nabiha herself have been transformed through the encounter with Lizzy and her persuasions, in spite of what ultimately happened to the baby?

6) 'If like Nabiha your experience is of a religion of submission and acceptance and life's painful trauma must be accepted as the will of almighty Allah, then to be told "God loves you" is meaningless.' Is that true? Does this encapsulate one of the most vital points of difference between Christianity and other religions (in this case Islam)? In other words, if Nabiha had been a Christian, would it have been possible for Lizzy to say those words and for them to have had meaning and comfort in a way she thought was impossible at the time? In any case, did Lizzy need to feel so bad about not being able to say the words, since everything she had done and said in the preceding weeks had actually been expressing their truth?

You might try to role-play this story, taking the parts of: Lizzy; the cleaner; other nurses; Nabiha; and the man from the orphanage.

### Three for the Price of One

1) What more could have been done to prevent the sad outcome of this story? If your answer is 'Nothing' how would your reaction be different from that of Habiba – 'Maktub' – it is written, and must be accepted as God's will?

2) The 'real' cause of the deaths, of course, in our under-standing, was human ignorance and error (as so often,

well-intentioned). How does that fit with a Christian understanding of 'God's will', and the Islamic interpretation expressed in Habiba's words?

3) If one is going to work at all in situations of much suffering and apparently preventable disease and death, should one put the question 'Who is to blame?' firmly to one side? Or is that merely capitulation to passive acceptance?

## Friendship's Heart of Hospitality

1) Religion and culture are so often the source of hostility and hatred. Yet here the warmth of friendship clearly transcended both barriers. From a Christian point of view, does this say something about the power of love, about the image of God in all human beings of whatever religion or culture? And what implications do such reflections have on the neat categories that we usually want to use when discussing the agendas of 'Christian mission'?

2) Lizzy found new meaning in the biblical tradition of sacrifice in the Old Testament, and its application to the death of Jesus Christ in the New Testament through her experience of Islamic sacrifice and the slaughter of a lamb at a picnic. Is our western understanding of the Christian faith too sanitized and cerebral? Ought we to find more challenging contextual symbols to give expression to its central truths, and if so, what might they be?

3) How could Lizzy have used her insights to help Safia to understand the heart of her Christian faith?

4) Many Christians have great reservations about any kind of 'inter-faith worship'. Yet in the context of the great pain of bereavement and shared grief among family and friends, Lizzy joined in the prayers at the Amri home. What was she expressing by doing so? What would she have communicated if she had not done so?

5) 'As a Christian I could find fulfilment in my singleness but it just wasn't there for a North African Muslim girl.' This

statement has both religious and cultural depths. What do you think Lizzy meant? Is singleness in fact any easier: a) for a Westerner than for a North African? b) for a Christian than for a Muslim? How and why?

## General Questions Relating to the Whole Book

1) What insights and reflections have you found that this book raised on the question of suffering in the world? How has your response to such suffering been challenged?

2  'But if we can discover how God feels for our hurting society, his empowerment will make a lasting difference. Come to think of it, it's rather like duet-playing! For the master musician's heart breaks when he sees us stamp, squeeze, wring and blast life from each other and he extends an invitation to join his lament. But playing the second violin isn't easy.' What is your assessment of Lizzy's concluding picture drawing together insights gained through these stories of 'living separation'? How would you view this as a valid and realistic response to our suffering world?

3) In what way has this book challenged or sharpened your understanding of God, of people, of mothers, of medical practitioners, of relief and aid workers, etc.?

4) What issues have been raised for you regarding the clash of cultural assumptions and beliefs? In what way has the book challenged your view of 'Western' and 'Islamic' cultures?

5) Similarly, what issues have been raised for you regarding the clash of religious assumptions and beliefs? In what way, particularly, has it enabled you to see the implications of Christian beliefs through contrast with those of Islam?

6) It is easy to have a romantic and sentimental view of relief and medical aid work – all those kind people going to help the poor refugees, etc. In what way has the book made you rethink that picture? What are the tensions and conflicts that such work entails, and what kind of qualities and training do people need who get involved in it?

7) How do you respond to the constant irony of the book that contrasts the frequent 'failure' of Western resources, skills and power, with the deeper 'success' of personal love, friendship and commitment? What does this say to strategies which see mission mainly in terms of management, problem-solving, technology, etc? What does it say also to the western obsession with quick and measurable results from simple short-term projects?

8) In the same way how do you respond to the paradox of the book in which Lizzy sees being a 'Cracked Pot' as something positive? How does this contrast with a western obsession with professional success, achievement, and building of personal empires?

9) Discuss the assertion that Lizzy gained access to certain countries or situations only because of her professional skills, and yet her success in personal 'mission' was often in spite of them, or at least in situations where they were useless.

10) The expression, 'The Lord has given and the Lord has taken away; blessed be the name of the Lord' is often used by Christians in the context of death and bereavement. In fact it comes from the book of Job. Job is honoured as a prophet within Islam. Is there any way in which such an affirmation could be used in relation to the stories of this book without it being simply a statement of painful submission to the will of Allah? How can its wider biblical context enable it also to be a statement of hope?

11) Lizzy sometimes reflects on all the immense resources that would have been available to her in a Western maternity hospital for which she had been trained, in contrast with the meagre resources and decidedly unhygienic situations she had to cope with in her work. Is it appropriate to compare that to the incarnation? The Son of God, accustomed to all the resources of his infinite power with God the Father, coped with all the limitations of an earthly life and its culture, religious and physical stresses, in order to be able to serve and give his life for people. In what other forms of mission does this 'incarnational principle' have particular relevance?

12) Lizzy is a Christian. She believes and lives and wants to share the transforming love God has shown her. But she has worked, and still works, in situations where that is difficult to do in a verbal or public form. How do you evaluate the Christian content and focus of her work as expressed in these stories? Do they illustrate the view that mission is more than the spoken word? Or do they fall short of what you would classify as true mission?

13) Some of the stories raise ethical problems and dilemmas. For example, you may have been upset at the treatment of women, at female circumcision, at the attitude to mothers who cannot produce male children or who have repeated still-births, etc. What principles (biblical or theological) can be used to address the problem that some things are viewed as right and normal in one culture but as cruel and demeaning in another?

14) When such conflicts did occur in some of the stories, Lizzy felt that her only alternative, given her situation, was to stand aside as the outsider and allow the local custom and culture to have its way, even though it caused her great pain. Is there ever a case for a more interventionist stance? It may not be for midwives to try to change the course of history (though the two in Exodus 1 played such a role!), but is there a place for other Christians, or the Church corporately, to speak and act in the social, political and international arenas in order to try to change practices that hurt or demean people – especially marginalized groups? Is that also a valid dimension of mission?

15) Several of the stories are set around the time of Good Friday and Easter, and the relevance of the setting is brought out. In what way would you see that as the enduring message of the whole book: suffering and death, leading on to resurrection and glory? How would you apply that profound biblical combination, so much at the very heart of the whole Christian message, to other situations of suffering known to you, to the world in general, and to the priorities of Christian mission?